Leslie has been trusted with company secrets, but is there anyone who Leslie can trust?

"I need to ask you something related to my job."

"Fire away," Hampton said pleasantly.

Leslie raised her head and stared into his blue eyes. "A page is missing from my VIRCO printout. Did you take it?"

For a moment Hampton resembled a statue frozen in time, his coffee cup suspended near his mouth, his eyes staring back into hers with shocked surprise. Then he looked away as he set his cup down on the table without drinking from it. "What makes you ask?"

"You were there. You handled it."

"Therefore I must be guilty."

"You haven't answered me," Leslie said, her cheeks warming. "A simple yes or no will do."

"I don't suppose pleading the Fifth Amendment would help, would it?"

"Not if you've already incriminated yourself."

"Have I done that?" Hampton's eyes locked on hers, his message clear.

KAY CORNELIUS lives in Huntsville, Alabama, the setting for *A Matter of Security*. Mrs. Corneluis' talent for research and detail brings her stories to life. Her "Frontiers of Faith" historical series has been one of **Heartsong Presents** most popular series.

Books by Kay Cornelius

HEARTSONG PRESENTS
HP60—More Than Conquerors
HP87—Sign of the Bow
HP91—Sign of the Eagle
HP95—Sign of the Dove

A Matter
of Security

Kay Cornelius

Heartsong Presents

To my husband, Don—*who also happens to be my best friend*—*with thanks for his unfailing love, understanding, and support for many wonderful years.*

Don's work—*with the U.S. Army at Redstone Arsenal, with NASA at the Marshall Space Flight Center, and now with Lockheed Missiles and Space Company in Huntsville*—*is typical of that of thousands of men and women like him whose contributions to the space industry have made possible numerous scientific advances and bettered countless lives right here on our own home planet.*

A note from the Author:
I love to hear from my readers! You may write to me at the following address: **Kay Cornelius**
                                    Author Relations
                                    P.O. Box 719
                                    Uhrichsville, OH 44683

ISBN 1-55748-699-9

A MATTER OF SECURITY

Cover illustration by Brian Bowman.

PRINTED IN THE U.S.A.

one

Leslie Christopher pulled her blue Toyota into the parking lot of ArrowSpace/South, turned off the ignition, and stared at the imposing red brick building before her.

It was still hard for Leslie to realize that she was about to become a project manager, a position that few women—and certainly none who had barely turned thirty—had ever held in the history of the huge ArrowSpace company.

Everything had moved so quickly that it still seemed somehow unreal. Leslie had been looking forward to a few days off after working as deputy on a project at Vandenburg Air Force Base when David Douglass, their division director, had told her she had been selected to fill an opening at ArrowSpace/South. Leslie had applied for it almost automatically, without any idea that she would get it and without any inkling what Huntsville, Alabama, the location of ArrowSpace/South, would be like. But once she had been offered the job, Leslie hadn't hesitated to take it. She had no personal ties to Los Angeles, no one to beg her to stay there. And for her career, it was definitely the right move.

Leslie reached for the new burgundy leather briefcase that her co-workers had given her at a farewell party and hoped she looked more confident than she felt. Her initial excitement over winning the management position had faded, leaving her to consider sober reality. Suppose she couldn't handle the pressure? Leslie imagined the possible consequences of failure—demotion and returning to Los Angeles in disgrace at best, dismissal from the company at worst—and shuddered.

"No!" she exclaimed, shaking her head as if to clear it. She wouldn't allow herself such thoughts. This would be a tough job, but she could handle it. Over the last nine years, Arrow had invested a great deal in Leslie, paying for her master's degree and moving her into positions of ever-increasing responsibility. They would never have sent her here if they didn't think she could do the job.

Leslie squared her shoulders, took a deep breath, and all but marched up the long walkway to the ArrowSpace/South main entrance.

⤳

Sitting in the ArrowSpace waiting room, Hampton Travis was bored. For the tenth time that morning he looked at his watch. It gave the time in any part of the world, computed the elapsed time between any two events, and performed arithmetic and algebraic calculations. But it couldn't tell him when he would be summoned by ArrowSpace's frosty receptionist. Hampton opened his briefcase and removed a slender file folder containing his resumé and Arrow's most recent advertisement for engineers and physicists. Dozens of such notices appeared in newspapers all over the country. Most of them, like the one to which he was responding, were placed by companies which planned to bid on lucrative contracts. The winning company would have good jobs to offer for the duration of the project, often many years. Losing companies threw the resumés away, so engineers usually applied to many firms.

Hampton glanced over his resumé, satisfied that it would impress any Arrow project manager. As an ex-astronaut, he had all the right credentials. And if all else failed, there were strings to be pulled to get him in to do the job he had to do. But for now, he knew he was simply one of many applicants seeking an interesting position.

Hampton had just closed his briefcase when he heard the receptionist speak. He half rose, assuming that she was summoning him, only to see her talking to a trim young woman in a periwinkle blue suit. She had honey-blond hair, worn just below her shoulders in the back and short around her oval face. He noted with approval that the skirt of her strictly business suit was modestly long, and that she was, indeed, an attractive young woman. She smiled at the receptionist and said something that Hampton was too far away to hear, but he liked the sound of her voice. A new executive secretary, perhaps, he thought; he doubted that she was an engineer.

The receptionist pointed toward the elevators, and the young woman moved toward them with an easy, unaffected stride. Then Hampton noticed that she had left a briefcase on the floor by the desk. Picking it up, Hampton hurried after her.

"I believe this may belong to you," he said.

Leslie turned to see a man with very dark hair and startlingly blue eyes holding out her briefcase. His smile appeared genuine—he didn't seem to be making fun of her forgetfulness—and Leslie smiled back and thanked him.

"I would have wondered where it was," she said, realizing even as she spoke that it wasn't a particularly brilliant remark.

"Now you won't have to."

Before Leslie could think of anything else to say, the elevator arrived and Leslie entered it. As the doors closed, the man lifted his hand in a lazy salute.

I must be more nervous than I thought to leave my brief-case like that, Leslie thought. She wanted to make a good first impression, but she feared she hadn't made a very good start.

"I'm Leslie Christopher from the Los Angeles office," she told the Special Projects administrative aide a few moments later, when she finally located the office.

"Sally Hanover," the woman said, offering her hand in a firm shake. Leslie judged her to be in her early forties, perhaps, with frosted blond hair and tasteful, understated makeup. Her charm bracelet jangled as she spoke into the phone, then turned back to Leslie. "Mr. Meredith wants you to report to Personnel and get badged. I'll take you there." Sally added, seeing Leslie's hesitation, "This building can be rather confusing."

As they walked to the elevator, Sally began telling Leslie where the cafeteria was—"not that anyone can eat the food"—and where the best parking spots were—"you have to ask, they won't assign you one unless you do." Leslie knew she had found someone who knew the really important things about ArrowSpace/South, Huntsville Division.

"Are you married?" Sally asked unexpectedly, and Leslie shook her head. "Well, watch out for the guys around here," she said. A young mail clerk riding in the elevator with them grinned at Leslie.

"Don't pay her no nevermind," he said. "She couldn't catch herself a man with a rope."

"There, see what I mean?" Sally punched the boy on his arm as the elevator doors opened and he pushed his mail cart down the hall. "Actually, I caught the only man I ever wanted when I was eighteen. . .Jeff. But he died several years ago," Sally said more seriously. "Of course, he wasn't an engineer—as a lot, they make poor husbands."

"So I hear," Leslie said, thinking of some of the engineers she had known in Los Angeles, men so wrapped up in their own work that they hardly knew other people existed, much less how to deal with them.

"Here you are," Sally said at the door to Personnel. "I'll leave you in Mrs. Garrett's clutches. Oh, I almost forgot—welcome to Arrow."

"Thank you," Leslie said. Sally walked away, her heels clicking on the waxed tiles in time with the clink of her bracelet.

"That one's a real card," Mrs. Garrett said dryly. "Transfer or new hire?"

"Transfer," Leslie replied, somewhat deflated that she hadn't been expected. "I have my file with me."

"Give it to me and fill out these papers." Mrs. Garrett handed Leslie a clipboard bearing a sheaf of pages. "You can sit over there," she added, waving to a table to the right of the receptionist's desk.

Leslie wanted to tell the woman that all the information the forms requested, except for her local address and telephone, was already in the file, but she knew the bureaucratic drill well enough to realize she would only be wasting her breath.

Leslie had just written "deceased" in the blanks that

asked about her parents when she heard a pleasant male voice and looked up to see the man who had returned her briefcase talking to Mrs. Garrett. He wore a visitor's badge and held a black briefcase. Her first impression—that he was a very handsome man and knew it—was reinforced as he smiled at Mrs. Garrett, who smiled back almost as if against her will. Leslie watched to see if he would also be given papers to fill out, but apparently he was there on other business, for after a brief conversation that Leslie could not hear, he walked away. The man never looked her way, and she certainly had no reason to think that he would speak to her if he had. But Leslie was curious and asked about him when she returned her papers.

"He looks familiar," Leslie added as Mrs. Garrett regarded her coolly.

"His name is Hampton Travis. He's not currently working here."

"Oh, I see. I don't suppose I know him, after all. What next?"

Mrs. Garrett handed Leslie a slip of paper. "Take this to the second door on the left. They'll make you an ID badge."

To Leslie's relief the young, crew-cut photographer was much more pleasant than Mrs. Garrett had been.

"You can smile for this, you know," he told her when she stood before the camera. "You may not feel much like smiling after you get to know this place."

Like most people she had met so far, including the manager of her apartment complex, the photographer spoke with a distinct southern inflection, and she smiled in spite of herself as he snapped the shutter.

"Is working here really that bad?"

"It beats unemployment, but you do have to look out for yourself."

Leslie would have asked what he meant, but the clerk who would make the badge motioned for Leslie to follow her into another room where the photo was laminated. *I look like a simpering half-wit*, Leslie thought when she saw the shot. Deftly the girl attached a clip and handed it to Leslie.

"This is a temporary badge. When you get security clearance, you'll get a permanent one. Any questions?"

Leslie shook her head. When she made no move to put on the badge, the clerk prompted her to do so in the tone of a mother to a backward child. "Security's very strict here," she added sternly.

With her badge safely in place, Leslie was allowed to return to the fifth floor. Sally Hanover's smile was friendly as she welcomed Leslie back, but her news was disappointing.

"Mr. Meredith has been called to a meeting upstairs. He sends his apologies and suggests that you take a long coffee break."

"When can he see me?"

Sally shrugged. "Sometimes these front-office sessions last through lunch, or he could be back in fifteen or twenty minutes. You might as well have coffee while you wait. Take the elevator down to the basement and follow your nose. But watch those sweet rolls—they're lethal."

None of the several dozen people in the cafeteria paid Leslie any attention as she took her coffee to an empty table. She felt uncomfortable as she had so many times throughout her childhood, always the new girl sitting by herself as her father followed elusive job leads from town to town.

But this is different, Leslie told herself; even though she knew no one, she belonged here. The dining area was decorated with huge murals of the Saturn V moon rocket, the Space Shuttle *Endeavor*, and the Space Station, three of the many NASA projects in which ArrowSpace had played a major role. She felt a quiet pride that she was about to join such a prestigious team.

Leslie hadn't been in the cafeteria very long when she again saw the briefcase man, as she thought of him— Hampton Travis, Mrs. Garrett had called him. *His name is familiar*, Leslie thought, but she couldn't make a connection. He stood in the door and looked around as if searching for someone. He glanced at Leslie, then looked again in a classic doubletake. She lowered her head, not wanting to let him see her staring at him, and when she looked up again, he was talking to a slender woman who wore her almost-black hair in a shoulder-length pageboy cut. The woman took his arm in a familiar way, as if she were accustomed to walking with him, and they left the cafeteria. Had he really noticed her? Or had she so expected that he would that she had imagined his interest?

Don't be stupid, Leslie, she lectured herself sternly. She hadn't come to Arrow to ogle men, but to take a responsible job that would require her full attention. Whoever Hampton Travis was, she couldn't allow him—or anyone else—to distract her.

❧

Thirty minutes later, Leslie was being ushered into Mr. Meredith's office and Hampton Travis was leaving Personnel with a last smile for Mrs. Garrett.

"Don't look at me like that, Barbara," Hampton admonished the brunette who almost matched his five feet, ten inch height and who walked with him toward the main entrance. "The Personnel woman may be a real dragon, but I want her on my side."

Barbara looked annoyed. "You don't really have to go through channels at all. A word in the right place, and..."

"You know that wouldn't do," Hampton said. "Everything has to be open and above board, or it won't work."

"But suppose you aren't hired?" Barbara asked.

They reached the door and stopped. Hampton glanced over at the bored security guard, then back to Barbara.

"I won't worry about that yet. You have your job. Do it, and let me worry about mine."

"But—" she began.

"No, Barbara. This is my show, remember? I'll be in touch."

Hampton returned his visitor's badge to the security guard and left the building before she could reply. Outside, the warmth of the sun reminded him that it would be another hot Alabama day. Hampton sighed and wished that he didn't have to deal with Barbara—she could be difficult.

As he got into his Thunderbird, Hampton thought briefly of the pretty blonde he had seen that morning and wished, not for the first time, that he had never agreed to undertake this particular assignment.

⁂

Mr. Meredith stood as Leslie entered his office. A large-framed man whose loose clothing suggested a recent weight loss, he extended his hand for a firm handshake and motioned her to be seated.

"I'm sorry you had to wait, Miss Christopher, but one of the first things you learn around here is that when the top floor calls, you answer."

Leslie nodded. "I took your advice and went to the cafeteria, which is probably the only part of the building I could find again."

"Yes, these windowless wonders are difficult, but you'll soon find the shortcuts. Have you found a place to live yet?"

"Yes, I've taken an apartment at the Willows. I'll be at the Guest Inn until my furniture arrives."

"If there's anything I can do to help you get settled, please let me know."

"Thank you, but so far everything has gone very well."

That's enough small talk. Now tell me about my job, Leslie thought.

He was silent for a moment, then he leaned back in his chair and picked up a Shuttle-shaped letter opener, turning it in his hands as he spoke. "I know you're curious about the project you'll be working with. I wish you could begin right away, but we must wait for your security clearance."

Leslie looked surprised. "I have clearance—I'm sure that must be on my record."

"Indeed, yes," Mr. Meredith agreed, "but that was obtained when you first went to work for Arrow. You'll need the highest clearance here. Until it comes through, you can rotate through every office you'll interface and meet some of the people you'll be dealing with. Then you'll be in a better position to manage your project."

Leslie wet her lips and leaned forward. "Can you tell me something about it now? Mr. Douglass said it was important, but that's all he told me."

"He knew a little, but I asked him not to discuss it with you, and this is not the time to go into the details. But as you know, this is different from our usual work."

"Mr. Douglass said it concerned a joint Pentagon and NASA project."

"That's at least partly correct—" Mr. Meredith started to speak, then frowned as if he had just thought of something unpleasant.

Leslie sensed that her new boss wished that Arrow had chosen someone else—someone older, more experienced, and, above all, male—to fill her position.

"There's one thing you should probably know from the start." Mr. Meredith chose his words with care. "You weren't the only person considered for this job. In fact, many might argue that you weren't even the most qualified candidate. Some of our local people resent being passed over. I hope no one will give you a hard time, but I think you should be aware of the situation from the start."

Leslie nodded, feeling a chill at his words. Perhaps unspoken was Mr. Meredith's own reluctance to have her instead of someone he already knew. It was common knowledge that Arrow had been sued by a woman in their Long Island facility who claimed that qualified women were not being considered for enough management positions. The case had been settled out of court, but Leslie had no doubt that it had some influence on her rapid advancement in Los Angeles. It could also explain why she had been chosen to fill this job as well. The thought was not comforting.

"Thank you for telling me," Leslie said.

Mr. Meredith nodded curtly and reached for the telephone. "I'll ask Sally to show you around a bit. You can begin meeting the people in Design tomorrow."

"How long will it be before I can start to work?" Leslie asked, disappointment clear in her tone.

"That depends on the FBI, but it shouldn't take more than a few days or so—and in the meantime, you'll be learning things that will help you do the job."

"I understand that, and I'm looking forward to meeting everyone. But I had expected to go to work right away."

"Exactly the way I'd feel in your place," Mr. Meredith said as he escorted her to the door of his office.

૨ઢ

Leslie thought that no work she could ever do in her life would be as hard as the days she spent at Arrow *not* working. In spite of Mr. Meredith's wish for her to rotate through other offices, everyone seemed to be busy, and once she had met them, no one knew quite what to do with her. Her chief accomplishment was learning the layout of the building, much of which would remain off-limits until she got the proper clearance. She met many people, few very impressive. All in all, it was such a waste of time that Leslie was glad when her furniture arrived and she had an excuse to take a few days off to get moved into her apartment.

"Go ahead," Mr. Meredith said, seeming to be equally relieved that she had something else to occupy her mind. "I'll call if we need you."

On the way out, Leslie stopped to tell Sally that she was leaving.

"Do you have any plans for Sunday?" Sally asked. "I'd like to come by for you and take you to my church."

"Your church?" Leslie repeated, as if surprised to think of Sally in connection with any of the churches she had noted around Huntsville.

"Yes—Glenview. The singles group there has been my lifesaver."

Leslie hadn't been to a church in years, and the thought of joining a widow Sally's age in a singles group wasn't at all appealing. "Thanks for the invitation, but I really do need to work all weekend to get my apartment in shape."

Sally looked disappointed. "I'll give you a rain check, then," she said.

Leslie nodded. "Maybe some day," she murmured. *But more likely, never. I'm not ready to go looking for a man just yet,* Leslie thought. She had never gone to a singles bar in California, but she supposed that if a woman had to have male companionship, a church might be as good a place as any to find it.

Grateful to have something to do, Leslie attacked the business of settling into her apartment. She bought a telephone and had it hooked up, and on an impulse she dialed her old office.

"Leslie! How's the South? You taken your shoes off yet?" teased Alice Morrison, who had been Leslie's best friend at Arrow/West.

"The South is fine, and everyone I've seen so far has shoes—even a few Gucci loafers," Leslie replied.

"Your old job hasn't been filled yet, and we miss you. Want to come back?"

Leslie pictured Alice sprawled at her desk, muttering under her breath every time her computer beeped at a command it didn't like, and smiled. "No, thanks. I think my California bridges are pretty well burned."

They talked for a few more minutes, then Leslie hung up. She was glad she'd made the call, but despite the frustration she had encountered in her new job, Leslie was still not sorry she'd left Los Angeles.

Leslie had just replaced the receiver when the doorbell rang, and she opened the door to a man of medium height with graying hair and wire-rimmed spectacles.

"Miss Christopher? I'm Special Agent Jack Taylor, with the FBI," he said, displaying a badge. "I need to ask you a few questions, if this is a convenient time."

"Of course—come in." Leslie moved a stack of towels so he could sit down.

"I understand that you work for ArrowSpace/South, Huntsville Division?"

Leslie nodded. "I can't imagine what else the FBI would need to know about me. I had clearance in Los Angeles."

"Yes, I know. We just need to update your file."

He wrote in a notebook as Leslie answered several routine questions, then when she thought he had finished, he had one more. "Is there anyone who works for the Federal government or its contractors on secret matters with whom you have a personal relationship?"

"No," Leslie said quickly. *I had no personal relationships in Los Angeles at all*, she thought. It was one reason that leaving it had been so easy.

He nodded and closed his notebook. "That's all we need. Thank you for your time."

"When will I have my clearance?" Leslie asked at the door.

"By the first of next week, if everything checks out."

"Thanks. I'll look forward to that."

Feeling somewhat cheered that at least a start had been made on her clearance, Leslie returned to her unpacking, humming under her breath. When the doorbell rang again late that afternoon, Leslie's first thought was that the FBI agent must have thought of something else and returned, and she opened the door without first looking through the peephole.

Leslie was startled to see Hampton Travis—and a little surprised that she hadn't forgotten his name—at the door. Leslie was suddenly and painfully aware that her hair needed combing and that her nose was probably shiny and that she didn't want him to see her when she was in such a mess. But it was too late—there he stood on her doorstep, his blue eyes opened wide and his mouth an "O" of surprise as she opened the door.

"Is your husband at home?" he asked.

"My husband?" Leslie repeated.

"Yes, Leslie Christopher, who works for ArrowSpace."

"Leslie Christopher is not my husband," she said.

Hampton rubbed his chin, which had a charming cleft right in the middle, and looked embarrassed. "I'm sorry to disturb you, but I wanted to see Leslie Christopher about a work-related matter, and I was given this address. I suppose I got some incorrect information."

Leslie had momentarily relished his discomfort, but now she felt guilty and hastened to end the misunderstanding. "My name is Leslie Christopher, and I do work at Arrow. Did they give you my address?"

"Well, not exactly. I asked someone who works there to

find out who would manage a project I'm interested in, and your name turned up. Directory assistance did the rest."

"And told you I was a man?"

"No. I did that on my own," he said with such an engaging smile that Leslie had no choice but to return it.

"So here you are, Mr. Travis," she said.

His face registered surprise, then a dawning recognition. "I saw you at Arrow, didn't I?"

"Yes. You rescued a briefcase I left behind the first day I was there."

"So that's why your face is so familiar," he said. "I came here to ask Mr. Christopher to discuss the new project with me over dinner. Since he doesn't seem to live here, will Miss Christopher dine with me in his place?"

The logical, sensible part of her mind told Leslie she ought to refuse his invitation, but the part that had found him attractive from the first urged her to accept. Without letting herself think through all the possible consequences, Leslie found herself agreeing.

"But I can't go anywhere like this," she added, glancing down at her well-worn jeans and ancient UCLA sweatshirt.

"I'll come back in an hour, then," he offered.

"I'll be ready," Leslie said, but for what, she wasn't so sure.

As she showered, Leslie tried to imagine what it would be like to work with Hampton Travis. At the moment, he seemed to know more about her job than she did—and it intrigued her to think that he might give her information that her own boss hadn't.

I cannot become interested in him personally, Leslie

told herself. She had vowed to succeed as a project manager, and succeed she would, with no frivolous romantic involvements to get in her way. Hampton Travis would be a good business contact, period.

But Leslie had to admit that it certainly didn't hurt that he was also one of the most attractive men she had ever met.

two

Leslie wasn't sure what she should wear for a business dinner. After standing before her closet for some time, she chose a simple black skirt and an oversized silk shirt, and topped it with a single gold chain. Understated and safe.

When she opened the door to Hampton again, the admiration in his eyes told Leslie that she had chosen well. As he held the car door for her—a nice gentlemanly touch, she thought—she deliberated telling him that she probably shouldn't have agreed to have dinner with him.

"If you think I can talk about anything that is going on at Arrow, you're wrong. I don't even know what I'm going to be doing. On the other hand, I'll be glad to hear anything you might know about it."

Hampton glanced at her and narrowed his blue eyes as if he doubted her. "That would be quite a switch, wouldn't it? The thing is, we ought to be acquainted, anyway—someone should welcome you to Huntsville. Just think of this evening in that light, and enjoy yourself."

"Where are we going?" Leslie asked. They had passed the gaudy restaurant row on University Drive and were heading west to an area Leslie had never seen.

"Trust me," he said. "One of my main areas of expertise is knowing where to find good food."

"You're not from around here, are you?" Leslie asked as he turned off the main highway onto a narrow asphalt road.

"What makes you think that?"

"The way you talk—definitely no Southern drawl."

"What is the idear of this inquisition?" Hampton said, adopting a broad Southern accent. "Ahr you makin' fun of the way Ah speak?"

"No, just trying to place it. I've lived a lot of different places, and I can usually guess what section of the country people are from. But you're a real challenge."

"Let's leave it that way for now. Here we are."

Hampton turned the car into a long driveway edged with huge, ancient boxwoods, pungently fragrant in the cool evening air. An old house, with white columns shining in the dusk, stood at the end of the driveway. A few automobiles were parked to one side, and a small sign identified the place as the Stagecoach Inn, ca. 1855.

"It's lovely!" Leslie exclaimed as Hampton opened her door. A white jacketed maitre d' bowed to them at the entrance and smiled broadly at Hampton.

"I wondered when we'd see you again. You been away a long time, Mist' Travis."

"Yes, I was out of town for a while, Joseph. This is Miss Christopher, who is new to Alabama. She's from —" He stopped, and Leslie realized she hadn't told him.

"I'm from the South too—Southern California," she said.

"Believe me, it's not the same South," Hampton said. "Joseph, shall we show the lady some real Southern hospitality?"

"Oh yes, sir, we'll have to do that." Joseph looked at Leslie as if he pitied her unfortunate origins. "Right this way."

Two large rooms of the inn had been refurbished,

forming the dining area. The very formal room was accented with antique buffets and sideboards, and every table was covered with the finest damask and set with sparkling crystal and translucent porcelain. Although there were empty tables in the dining room, Joseph led them through it and seated them on a veranda at the rear, overlooking a small lake. With a pale moon rising in the darkening sky, it could have been a movie set. Leslie had never seen anything remotely like the place.

"It's almost like traveling back in time," she said.

"Wait until you taste the food. I didn't call ahead to see what they're serving tonight, but it's always good."

A waiter appeared to fill their water glasses, and another brought in bowls of cold soup. Just as they were finishing, a young girl wearing an old-South hoop-skirted gown came onto the porch, camera in hand.

"Smile, y'all," she said, pointing the camera at them.

To Leslie's surprise, Hampton spoke sharply to the girl, "We don't want a picture." He half rose as if he might escort her from the room or seize the camera, or both.

"As you like, sir," the girl said as she backed away in haste.

"What was that all about?" Leslie asked when the girl had left.

"Oh, it's just a silly thing they do to make a few dollars. When I'm eating, I want to left alone," he added, as if he feared that Leslie might think him a penny-pinching old grouch.

"Like an old dog with a bone?" Leslie suggested, trying for a light touch.

Hampton looked relieved. "Exactly," he said, and smiled again. "I've had all the publicity I ever want."

Before Leslie could ask him what he meant, their entrees arrived with a great deal of ceremony, and Leslie was content to enjoy the food in silence, occasionally asking Hampton about the dishes they were served.

"The sauce on the chicken was wonderful," she told the waiter as he cleared away their dinner plates. "What gives it such a distinctive flavor?"

"I don't know, ma'am. The cook don't allow nobody to see what-all goes in it."

"There seem to be all kinds of things around here that are top secret," Leslie said when the waiter left.

"It's the nature of the place. Around Huntsville, if you don't have a few secrets, you're not very important."

"I'll have to remember that," Leslie said.

The rising moon traced a silver path across the water. Joseph had brought a hurricane lamp to their table as the daylight faded, and now the candlelight cast wavering shadows around them.

What a setting for romance, Leslie thought, tempted for a moment to forget that ArrowSpace existed and give her attraction to Hampton free rein, letting it lead where it would. But then she remembered that she hadn't come here for personal reasons. *This is strictly business*, Leslie reminded herself.

"This has been a most unusual business dinner," she declared as they sipped coffee from delicate cups. "The question is, when will we get around to discussing business?"

"Why spoil a lovely evening?"

"I don't consider talking about my work spoiling anything," Leslie said. "I'm really curious to find out what I'll be doing here. If you know, I wish you'd tell me."

"There's something I have to know first," he said, and even though he was leaning back in his chair, she had the eerie feeling that he had moved closer.

"What is that?"

"How did you happen to know my name?"

"That's easy—the day you returned my briefcase, I saw you again at Personnel. I asked Mrs. Garrett who you were."

"You were there when I was talking to her?" he asked. "And later—that was you in the cafeteria, wasn't it?"

Leslie nodded. "It's your turn now. What do you know about my job?"

"You make me sound like a fortune teller," he said. "I don't believe in such things." Nevertheless, Hampton took her left hand and turned it palm up, as if studying its lines. "This is the hand of an attractive young woman who is about to begin an interesting association with a new technology. She will meet many hazards, but the rewards will be great."

"That's too general," Leslie said. "Tell me something specific."

"I'm afraid that's all for now," Hampton said, but he continued to hold her hand until Leslie withdrew it.

"Because you can't? Or because you won't?"

"Let's just say that this is neither the time nor the place for such a discussion."

"That's not fair! You said this would be a business dinner."

"And it has been. This is the way things work around here. You might as well get used to it."

"I seem to have a lot to learn," Leslie said.

"You'll be all right." Hampton studied her face closely

for a moment before he signaled the waiter for the check.

"I still expect to hear what you know," Leslie said, trying to salvage some faint command of the situation.

"In due time. In the meantime, I should get you home."

"Thank you for the dinner," Leslie said as he came around to pull out her chair. "Everything was wonderful."

"The pleasure is mine, Miss Christopher. I had planned to take Mr. Christopher to the Steak House, but I'm glad he wasn't there."

Leslie stood and took Hampton's arm as they left the restaurant. The evening had turned chilly, and the sky blazed with stars as they walked slowly to the car.

"Look at that beautiful sight," Hampton said, pointing to the heavens. "I always think of Psalm 19 when I see so many stars—'The heavens declare the glory of God.' People have been wondering about those stars for years, and we're the first generation that's going to be able to find out what's really going on out there. It's almost mind boggling, isn't it?"

"Yes, I suppose it is," replied Leslie, surprised that a technically minded man like Hampton Travis could quote from a Psalm and be so enthusiastic about the beauty of the skies. "Do you know much about astronomy?" she asked as he helped her into the car and closed the door.

"A little," he said, and Leslie thought he sounded amused.

"Just what is that you do?" Leslie asked. "Are you an engineer?"

Hampton started the car and backed out of the parking space before replying. "I've done a little bit of everything," he said. "I spent some time in the Air Force and I've worked for NASA and on several contracts."

"And now you're with Arrow?" she asked.

"Not exactly. When your project gets revved up, I hope to be a part of it. That is, if the program manager decides to hire me."

Leslie made no effort to hide her surprise. "In Los Angeles, project staffing isn't done by mid-level managers."

"In case you hadn't noticed, you're not in LA any more."

"I noticed," Leslie said stiffly, her curiosity piqued. How could Hampton Travis know so much more than she did about the project that she was supposed to be managing? A new thought struck her, and she turned to Hampton. "Did you apply for the job they gave me?"

Hampton laughed. "No, Miss Christopher, I'm no manager. See those?" He had taken the interstate spur that led into the city and now pointed to the Space and Rocket Center, where the Space Shuttle and a display of rockets gleamed ghostly white in the moonlight. "That's my background. These show where we've been. And over there is where space exploration is continuing," he added as they passed the research park where ArrowSpace/South, Huntsville Division, occupied a sprawling complex.

"It's really an exciting place to work, isn't it?" Leslie said softly. Sometimes it was easy to lose sight of what she was doing in the midst of the multitude of tiny details that made up the big picture, much as the thousands of pieces of a mosaic seem totally unrelated until they are joined. But every piece was important, even the most seemingly insignificant—and she was here to become part of it.

"Yes, it is," Hampton agreed, "and Huntsville is a good place to live as well."

"How long have you lived here?" Leslie asked.

Hampton didn't look at her. "I don't actually live in Huntsville permanently," he said.

"Surely you don't live in California!" she exclaimed, thinking that would be the crowning irony.

"Not really. I suppose you might say I'm one of those aerospace gypsies. We travel by airplane now instead of in caravans, but we're a pretty rootless bunch. We work a job, move on to another, finish it, and move on again."

"That sort of life is awfully insecure, isn't it?" Leslie said, reminded of the way she had felt as a child with the constant moves.

"My security doesn't come from this earth," he said.

"That sounds ominous," Leslie said. *Was he teasing her?*

They had left the interstate spur and were passing under a series of bright yellow street lights, and Leslie could see from Hampton's expression that he was serious. "It isn't at all ominous," he said. "My faith is the anchor of my life."

Why is this man so enigmatic? Leslie asked herself. Hampton Travis had taken her out for a wonderful meal, but he hadn't told her anything about her job or even about himself. *Either he has something to hide, he's trying to confuse me, or he's a very private person.*

"I don't suppose you'll tell me what that means, either," Leslie said. Hampton laughed at the resigned tone of her voice.

"I'll be glad to—but not now. I can see that you're tired. I'd like to show you some of the sights by day." Hampton pulled into the Willows apartment complex and shut off the engine. "How about taking a picnic lunch to the top of the mountain on Saturday if the nice weather holds?"

"Strictly business, of course?" Leslie asked, and he nodded solemnly.

"Of course. How about it?"

Leslie hesitated, not wanting to seem too eager to see him again. "Can I let you know?"

"Sure—I'll call you."

Hampton came around to open her door and they walked in silence from the parking lot, past the deserted pool, and up a single flight of stairs to Leslie's apartment.

"Thank you again for the evening," Leslie said as she fitted her key into the lock. As Hampton pushed the door open, Leslie thought for a split-second that he was going to follow her inside, but he merely waited on the threshold until she had turned on a light. He made no move to kiss her, and after he left, Leslie felt a little angry with herself for wishing that he had.

Hampton Travis might turn out to be a useful business associate, but for now, I mustn't let him be anything else.

Then another thought struck Leslie. *Why, for all I know, he might even be married!* He didn't wear a wedding ring, but then, neither did many men she knew. It hadn't occurred to her to ask. Maybe that was why he hadn't kissed her. Most of the men she had dated would have taken a friendly kiss for granted after taking someone out for such a sumptuous evening.

"Well, as long as I keep this strictly business, it won't matter," Leslie told the mirror as she brushed her teeth. At any rate, she was too tired to worry about it any more that evening.

Leslie quickly got ready for bed and was asleep almost as soon as her head touched the pillow. Along toward dawn she dreamed that she was on an airplane, about to sit down beside Hampton Travis, when a tall, faceless woman with long black hair materialized and beckoned to him. Without a glance at Leslie, Hampton got up and went to the woman, and they floated out of the plane in some sort of murky gray cloud. Leslie wanted to follow them, but her legs suddenly felt like lead, and when she tried to call out, no sound came out of her tight throat.

Leslie awoke, her mouth dry and her heart beating wildly. Gray light filtered in through the miniblinds at her bedroom window, and her luminous clock dial showed just past six. She climbed out of bed, went into the bathroom, and splashed cold water on her face. Then she went to the kitchen and started the coffee.

The morning paper lay on her doorstep and Leslie picked it up and turned the pages idly as she ate breakfast. Then suddenly a photograph all but leaped at her. It was of a couple she remembered seeing the night before at the Stagecoach Inn, no doubt taken by the girl who had attempted to snap their picture. Under the heading "Dining out in Huntsville," the caption said that Mr. and Mrs. Morgan Gilruth had celebrated their tenth wedding anniversary at the Stagecoach Inn. Leslie recalled how upset Hampton had seemed when the girl had pointed her camera at them. Was it because he didn't want his picture taken with her for business reasons? That seemed unlikely. But if Hampton had a personal reason—like having a wife, a fiancée, or a girl friend who might question that his business dinner had been with a woman and at a romantic place. . . That could be a very good reason for him to avoid the camera.

The rest of the morning, as Leslie hung the few pictures she owned and finished stocking her cabinets, she alternated between feeling foolish for suspecting him of deviousness and thinking that it would be even more foolish to see him again, even if he weren't married. By the time she stopped working long enough to eat a quick lunch, Leslie had decided to tell Hampton she couldn't go on Saturday, and just leave it at that.

When he called her that afternoon, the sound of his voice shook her resolve so much that she almost changed her mind, but she held firm. "I'm sorry, Hampton, but I can't make it on Saturday. Thanks for the invitation, though."

"Mind telling me why?" he asked, and Leslie thought he sounded genuinely disappointed. "I'll even provide the lunch."

"I've been thinking of what you said about possibly working with me at Arrow. I don't know my way around the Huntsville office yet, but in Los Angeles, I wouldn't see someone socially that I might be working with unless it was related to our business. It just doesn't look right."

"This isn't Los Angeles, and I can assure you that things aren't all that cut and dried here. It's perfectly all right for you to have a private life, you know."

Who would care if I did go out with Hampton Travis? Leslie asked herself. *Who would even know about it?* But it was no use.

"Not this weekend—maybe later," she said with what she hoped was the right mixture of firmness and regret.

"All right, but don't think you've heard the last of me, Miss Christopher."

"Is that a threat?" Leslie asked, knowing that is wasn't.

"More like a promise. Look, I'll probably see you around Arrow. But if you ever decide to go up on top of the mountain alone, be careful. People are always falling over the edge. The rocks are sharp, and it's a long way down."

"I'll remember that," Leslie said, and heard the click as he hung up the phone.

Leslie sat with the receiver in her hand for a long time before she replaced it. A lonely weekend stretched ahead, and for a moment she remembered Sally's invitation to attend her church. Then she thought of the strain involved with meeting so many new people and decided she wasn't that desperate to make new friends. And with any luck at all, she would be at work—really at work this time—on Monday. Maybe she would find out what she was up against—and more about the mysterious Hampton Travis, as well.

three

Sally looked up in surprise when Leslie came in just before eight o'clock on Monday morning. "We didn't really expect to see you today. You must have gotten settled in record time."

"I'm not completely finished, but I had no real reason to stay away any longer."

"I'm glad you came back today," Mr. Meredith said when she entered his office."

"The FBI paid me a visit last week," Leslie said.

Mr. Meredith nodded. "I know—I told the chief of the local office that you needed to be brought on board right away. Your clearance might even come in today. In the meantime, Sally will show you your office."

Her office was not what Leslie had expected. At ArrowSpace/West a project manager rated a rather large office with a carpeted floor and upscale furnishings. Her office at ArrowSpace/South had been hastily made by partitioning a larger office into two rooms, the other vacant for the moment—"For your lead technical staff person," Sally had said. Its sparse furnishings included a desk, two metal chairs, an oversized filing cabinet, a metal bookcase, and a coat rack. A computer terminal sat on the desk, flanked by a tall stack of manuals. All Arrow offices made heavy use of software programs, so Leslie wasn't surprised to see it. She switched on the computer, which immediately beeped and asked for a password she hadn't been given. She turned it off and flipped through some of the manuals and was relieved to see that the system was similar to the one she had been using.

Leslie had just finished stowing the manuals in her bookcase when Mr. Meredith summoned her to his office.

"Jack Taylor just called to confirm your clearance," Mr. Meredith said. "That means I can now tell you that you'll be working on Arrow's proposal for NASA's VIRCO project. I'm sure you must have heard something about it."

You can't be serious. Leslie's first thought was almost expressed aloud, but she managed to nod her head as if she had known it all along. There had been rumors for months that something really big was in the works, something that would bring lucrative contracts to the successful bidders. "It has something to do with unmanned space exploration, doesn't it?"

Mr. Meredith nodded. "That's a bit of an understatement. It calls for a completely new technology involving orbiting advanced virtual reality computers and robotics." He pointed to a formidable stack of documents. "Here's the outline of NASA's preliminary request for proposals. Read it carefully and you'll have an idea of the overt project."

Leslie reached for the bundle of papers and looked up questioningly at Mr. Meredith's use of the word "overt."

"I say that because the technology involved in this thing has many military applications as well—and that's why every company bidding on this contract and any foreign country who wants cheap space capability will be falling all over themselves to get a system together. Because Arrow already has a considerable base of expertise in these matters, we think we have the inside edge. But we must move fast, because many others also want this award—and they may have done more on it than we have."

Leslie looked again at the Request for Proposal, the "RFP" in the shorthand of the space business, and the words seemed to swim on the paper as she tried to make out the stated scope of the project. "It appears that NASA wants something very complex."

"Yes, and something that goes far beyond what we now think of as 'state of the art.' It will take an inter-disciplinary team of the very best scientists to win this bid."

"And it's our job to see that Arrow puts together such a team," Leslie said, understanding at least that much.

"Yes, and also to make sure that no one else knows the details of our proposal. Security is your top priority from now on."

Leslie was silent, feeling mingled excitement and fright that she would be playing a key role in such an important undertaking.

"I know you'll have questions after you review the material," Mr. Meredith said. "It's pretty overwhelming at first glance."

And at the second and third glance, too, Leslie thought. "I have never worked on anything this complex. I'm surprised that I got the job."

Mr. Meredith looked as if he wished she hadn't mentioned her inexperience. "That decision was made by others," he said, confirming Leslie's earlier suspicions. "Mr. Douglass assured me that you are a quick learner. I hope he's right."

"Thank you for your frankness," Leslie said with what

she hoped was the right tone. "I'll do my very best."

Mr. Meredith's nod was curt. "That's all anyone can ask. Now go back to your office and start reading every word of that RFP. And get Sally to help you with the computer system. You need to be up to speed with it as soon as possible."

"Is it still Monday?" Leslie asked as she and Sally shared an elevator at the end of the day.

"I'm afraid so. I see you didn't waste any time taking work home."

Leslie glanced at the proposal in her arms, too large to fit into her briefcase, and sighed. "I have a feeling taking work home might get to be a habit."

"You deserve a little fun," Sally said as the elevator reached the ground floor. "I can introduce you to some people from my singles group at church."

Fun with people from church? Leslie doubted it. "Thanks, but my life's complicated enough just now." Not wanting to hurt Sally's feelings, she added, "Later, maybe."

That night Leslie's mind replayed her interview with Mr. Meredith. *Security is your top priority from now on,* he'd told her, and Leslie knew that he meant seeing to it that nothing about their proposal ever got into anyone else's hands. But in a way, she reflected, "security" had always been her top priority, although she had never really managed to attain it. She'd thought that a good education and a stable job would make her feel secure, and for a while they had. But now, starting this formidable new task in a strange place, Leslie had never felt less secure.

I'll feel better when I've been here longer and am really accepted by everyone, she told herself.

After only a few days Leslie felt that she had been working on the VIRCO proposal for months. She came home
each night too exhausted to do more than have a quick
supper before wading through more reading and then falling into bed. She wouldn't have felt like going out, even
if she had been asked, but Hampton Travis hadn't called,
nor had she seen him around Arrow. Looking at her staffing charts, Leslie was reminded that he had told her he
had applied for a job at Arrow.

What would it be like to work with him? Leslie briefly
wondered, envisioning him working in the office next to
hers each day, taking care of the technical aspects of the
proposal. She quickly dismissed the thought as idle specu-
lation for which she had no time.

Still, when Leslie found Hampton waiting for her outside Arrow after work late one Monday evening, her heart
began to beat a bit faster.

"I hoped I'd catch you." He took her briefcase and fell
into step beside her like a schoolboy carrying his girl's
books home.

"What brings you to Arrow? I haven't seen you lately."

"Just checking. I have to go out of town for a few days,
and I wanted to make sure that you and Arrow don't forget me."

"Never!" Leslie exclaimed, matching his smile despite
her intention not to.

"Will you join me in a farewell dinner tonight?"

"I'm afraid I would be very poor company. I have so
much work to do—"

"Hey, you're not in school any more, remember? Tell
the truth, now—have you done anything for fun since you
got here?"

"I had dinner with you," Leslie said before she had time to think of how it might sound. "Learning my new job is fun enough for now," she added, then despaired. What must he think of her! Every time Leslie saw Hampton, she seemed to produce idiotic babble.

"You still have to eat, though."

"I'd have to get home early," Leslie said, weakening.

"I promise. My car is over here." He took her arm as they reached the curb and then seated her ceremoniously.

He knows a woman would have to be made of stone not to enjoy such attention, Leslie realized.

"We should go somewhere nearby," she said as they left the almost-empty Arrow parking lot.

"That's a project manager for you, always telling everyone what to do," Hampton said lightly.

"I'm very good at that," she agreed.

"We'll go to the Steak House, where I had intended to take Mr. Christopher. It's quite close."

When they arrived, Leslie was relieved to see that the atmosphere of the brightly-lit Steak House was much more utilitarian than romantic. Leslie noted that a large number of the diners were business-suited men.

"This place is a favorite of men who come here on TDY," Hampton said.

"Women never travel on temporary duty?"

He smiled. "Touché, Miss Executive. What would you like to have to eat?" he added as a waiter appeared to take their orders.

"What's good?"

"Beef, of course—the specialty of the house. Shall I order for us both?"

"By all means." Leslie folded her menu without looking at it. After a long day of making decisions, having someone else to do the thinking was a pleasant change.

"Tell me—what do you think of your new job, and how do you like Huntsville?"

"You've asked two completely different questions," Leslie said. "Huntsville seems to be a good place to live so far, although I haven't seen much of it. The work is the hardest I've ever had—and the most interesting."

"I thought you'd like it. But you're going to need some good help to get your proposal in on deadline."

Oh, no—here comes the job pitch, Leslie thought. "I am quite aware of that fact," she said stiffly.

"I wondered if you'd had a chance to look at my resumé yet."

"Your resumé?" Leslie repeated.

"I left it at Arrow the same day we met. I thought perhaps you had come across it by now."

His tone had changed only slightly, but Leslie picked up on it immediately. Now Hampton Travis was a man wanting a job which he thought she had the power to give him.

"I haven't seen any resumés yet," Leslie said truthfully enough; she had not really started staffing yet.

"Ask Personnel for it, then. Sometimes they can move with glacial slowness."

"I can't promise anything," Leslie said in her best professional voice. She avoided looking at him directly, not wanting him to see the disappointment in her eyes.

"I'm not asking for special treatment, but you won't find anyone more experienced in preparing the kind of bid that Arrow will need to make on this project."

Their salads arrived, and Leslie was grateful that Hampton seemed ready to concentrate on eating and drop the subject of his employment.

They had almost finished their steaks when Leslie noticed a tall, striking brunette enter the restaurant. She glanced over at them, then quickly looked away.

"Don't you know her?" Leslie asked, but by the time Hampton turned around to look, she was gone.

"What did she look like?"

"Tall, slender. I've seen her at Arrow."

Hampton looked amused. "I'm sorry to disappoint you, but I'm not acquainted with Arrow's entire female work force."

Is he telling the truth? Looking at him closely, Leslie decided that either Hampton was being honest, or he should take up acting professionally.

"That was the first steak I've had in ages," Leslie said as their plates were removed.

"Admit it—you've let this job keep you from eating properly."

"That's my concern, not yours," Leslie said with an edge of irritation. *The man can't have it both ways,* she thought. He was Hampton the job-seeker, or he was Hampton the charmer. She couldn't keep them straight in her own mind, much less know how to deal with them.

"Quite right, it is," he said, sounding properly chastened. "Shall we go?"

Hampton said little on the short drive back to Arrow. He parked next to her car and turned off the engine. "It may be a while before I see you again," he said when he came around to open her door. "I have to go out of town again."

Foolishly Leslie wished she could see his eyes, but the

darkness masked his expression. "When will you be back?"

"I don't know. Be careful, Leslie."

He had said the same thing to her before, she recalled. "I can take care of myself, thank you," Leslie said, then immediately regretted the prissy way it had sounded.

What is the matter with me? Leslie asked herself. She had held her own with some of the top scientists at Arrow/West, but Leslie seemed incapable of carrying on an even halfway intelligent conversation with Hampton Travis.

"I hope so," he said. "Well, I'll see you around."

Leslie had buckled her seat belt and started her motor before she realized she didn't have her briefcase. Quickly she rolled down her car window and called to him, "My briefcase is still in your car."

He stopped and nodded. "Oh—so it is." Hampton returned with it and handed it to her with a mock bow. "You can't afford to get careless with Arrow's papers," he said, then turned away before she could reply.

Strange, Leslie thought. Why had he felt the need to remind her of security considerations? She was quite aware she must be careful of the VIRCO material. She didn't need to be reminded of that—and most especially not by Hampton Travis.

&

The telephone was ringing as Hampton let himself into his apartment some fifteen minutes after leaving Leslie in the Arrow parking lot. He was not surprised to hear Barbara's voice at the other end of the line.

"What on earth do you think you are doing?" she asked as soon as he answered.

"Minding my own business, which is more than I can

say for you."

"Someone needs to mind it for you, apparently. You took Leslie Christopher out to dinner again—you can't deny it, because I saw you. What's more, she saw me, too."

"What's so bad about that? She asked me if I knew who you were, but by the time I turned around, you were gone."

"Great! I suppose I should have barged right in and joined you."

"I don't see why you're so upset. My strategy might change, but the aim is still the same."

"Just be sure you have the right target!"

Hampton winced, then shook his head as Barbara slammed down the receiver.

Women! Would he ever understand them? What had made a pro like Barbara Redmond behave like a jealous schoolgirl? And Leslie—

Well, she was a different matter. He thought he was making some progress with her. At least he hoped so. He would have to be very careful.

❧

"Guess what's waiting in your office," Sally said when Leslie came in on Thursday morning.

"I'm not up to games this early. Is it animate or inanimate?"

"Never mind—just enjoy it."

"I may not have time to enjoy anything today. Is my staff meeting still on for ten this morning?"

"Yes, and the material you asked me to copy is on your desk."

Leslie went down the hall and opened her office door to find a vase filled with a dozen red, long-stemmed roses sitting on her desk. The attached note, written in a bold, masculine hand, was brief: "Good luck with your new project—Hampton."

Leslie sat down hard in her desk chair and closed her eyes, half-believing that when she opened them, the roses would be gone. But they were not, and apparently, neither was Hampton Travis.

Flustered, Leslie threw the card into the wastebasket. What did he think he was doing, sending her flowers? Did he think he'd have the inside track for a job if he romanced her a little? Leslie was certain that if the VIRCO project manager were a man, Hampton wouldn't be sending him flowers.

"Men!" she said aloud. Then she set about getting ready for her first staff meeting, determined not to allow Hampton and his roses to rattle her composure.

"You've been holding out on me," Sally said later as she helped Leslie set up the conference room. "You must have met someone pretty special to be getting flowers like that."

"They don't mean what you think. I wish he hadn't sent them, as a matter of fact."

"You don't care for roses?"

"They overpower that small room. Would you like to put them on your desk, take them home with you tonight?"

Sally looked shocked. "I should say not! Listen, even if they came from Attila the Hun you ought to enjoy every whiff."

"I won't enjoy anything until after this meeting is over. I'm afraid Mr. Meredith already thinks that Arrow sent him an idiot."

"You'll do fine," Sally assured her.

Mr. Meredith entered the conference promptly at ten, looking a bit drawn. He nodded to Leslie and took a seat at the end of the table. A personnel specialist arrived to sit in on the meeting, along with the cost analyst and a systems engineer on loan from another Special Projects office.

After calling on the systems engineer to comment on VIRCO's complex engineering requirements, Leslie turned to the cost analyst. "Mr. Garner, what about the VIRCO budget?"

"Nothing's been worked up yet," the man said somewhat defensively.

"I know it's early yet—" Leslie began.

Mr. Meredith interrupted her. "Have you looked at what has been prepared so far?" The analyst nodded. "Then you should definitely have some figures on what each of the approaches will cost based on our previous experience with similar projects."

Mr. Meredith had not raised his voice, but there was no doubt that his displeasure had registered. Sam Garner made a few notes and promised to have some figures ready by the end of the week.

"Thank you," Leslie said. Embarrassed that Mr. Meredith had had to intervene, she hurried on to the next agenda item. "Concerning staffing, I've asked Mr. Birch to prepare a list of technical personnel already working here who might be able to help us ready the proposal. As you can see," she added, holding up the report, "the list is rather short. Is there anything else you can tell us today?"

Lowell Birch handed Leslie a folder containing several pages of information about engineers and consultants who had previously applied for work at Arrow. "This is all the computer search gave me. One problem is that we have no local pool of computer scientists. Ours are all busy, so we must look elsewhere."

"What about it, Mr. Meredith? Can we give the go ahead?" Leslie asked.

"We'll discuss it later," Mr. Meredith said, and once more Leslie had the distinct feeling that she had made a terrible mistake.

"Does anyone have anything else to bring up now?" Leslie asked. When no one responded, Leslie thanked them for coming and adjourned her first staff meeting.

"Let's go to my office." Mr. Meredith nodded toward the hall. Leslie gathered up her briefcase and followed her boss. She noticed that he seemed a bit less energetic than usual. He put an antacid mint into his mouth as he sat down at his desk.

"I didn't do very well, did I?" Leslie asked. "I thought I was ready, but it doesn't seem that much was accomplished."

"Everyone has to start somewhere," he said, not unkindly. "Next time make sure that you have a reason to meet. Have all material submitted to you in advance— staff meetings are no place for surprises."

"I know I have a lot to learn," Leslie said. "I'll be better prepared next time."

"I'm sure you will," he said, unsmiling. "Miss Christopher, I hadn't realized that you didn't do staffing in Los Angeles. Perhaps you need to be reminded that if there's a slot on the chart for a job, it must be filled as soon as possible. Funds are available for immediate hiring."

"Then I can tell Mr. Birch to start looking for computer geniuses?"

"You should already have been doing that. I assumed that you were. . . ."

Leslie sighed. "What else should I be doing that I haven't been?"

"The main thing is to get your staff together while the preliminary design team is working. And one more thing—"

"Yes?" The doubts she felt about her job performance were clear in both her face and her tone.

"Don't look so glum," Mr. Meredith said. "I know we don't do things the way you did them in Los Angeles, but you're trying, and I think you are willing to learn. But you absolutely must learn to be wary of everyone."

"Except for the people at Arrow, I know hardly anyone in Huntsville," Leslie said, not quite sure what Mr. Meredith meant.

"I'm sure as time passes that will change, as it should. Our business is very complicated, and it involves a great many people. We ought to be able to trust one another, but sometimes—well, it doesn't always work out that way. You must always be on guard."

Leslie waited for him to elaborate on the statement, but instead he stood, concluding their conversation. "Your first presentation is now history. Do your homework, and I can guarantee that the next one will be much easier."

"I hope so," Leslie said, but as she returned to her office, she doubted it. When she opened her door and the scent of roses engulfed her, Leslie felt a momentary pang of regret that Hampton wanted to work on VIRCO, complicating what might have possibly developed between them on a personal level.

That night Leslie had an early supper, then curled up

with the folder from Personnel on her lap and a note pad nearby, determined to make some progress in staffing. As Lowell Birch had mentioned, the few astrophysicists who already worked for Arrow were engaged in other projects. But there was one name listed—

"Hampton Travis," she said aloud, imagining his blue eyes smiling at her as his name all but leaped off the page. The information was quite sketchy; he had bachelor's and master's degrees in physics and a Ph.D. in computer science.

"He never told me he was a doctor," Leslie said aloud accusingly. Reading on, she saw that he had last worked for Arrow two years ago. His current occupation was "consultant," and his current address was a post office box. But there was a local telephone number.

"Okay, Dr. Travis," Leslie said, putting a checkmark by his name. "You're now on my official list."

Arrow needed a computer scientist, and he wanted a job. He had said he was going out of town, but perhaps he might be back. Dialing his number, Leslie felt strangely jittery. She recalled an incident in high school when she had worked up the nerve to call a boy she liked to invite him to a "backwards" party. She'd been so nervous she had hung up when she heard his voice, and she had never tried again. But things were different now. Leslie was an adult and this was a business call. She would be quite cool and professional.

Then a female voice answered, and at once Leslie felt a blind panic, imagining the tall brunette—probably his wife—on the other end of the line. Then reason returned, and Leslie asked to speak to Dr. Travis.

"This is his answering service," the voice said, and

Leslie felt an absurd surge of relief. "Dr. Travis is unavailable. Is there a message?"

"Please ask him to call Leslie Christopher," she said, and gave her office phone number.

Leslie returned to her list and made a few more calls, arranging for two engineers with appropriate experience to come in for interviews in the week ahead. By the time she had finished, Leslie felt far from confident about what she would say to Hampton Travis.

Only one thing bothered her: if they were to work together, she should never consider going out with Hampton again.

four

Friday began with the normal traffic tie-ups and extra congestion that usually occurred just before each weekend, and everything seemed to be headed downhill in a hurry as the day progressed. The scent of Hampton's roses permeated her office, making Leslie sneeze. She put the vase on Sally's desk and wished she had some way to air out her office.

Aggravation piled on aggravation as the day proceeded. The copying machine quit working, and copy work had to be taken to another floor, slowing down the paper flow and complicating Leslie's tasks. At midmorning came the news that Mr. Meredith would be out yet another day. He told Sally he was taking sick leave, but he didn't say what ailed him.

"I thought he looked pale at the staff meeting," Leslie said as she and Sally had lunch. "Did you notice it too?"

Sally nodded. "To tell the truth, I've been worried about his health for some time. He's lost a lot of weight lately, and whenever anyone says anything about it, he just makes a joke and says he's not eating as much junk food since Alicia—that's his daughter—went off to college."

"I hope he comes back soon," Leslie said. "I need his advice on so many things."

All day the pace continued to be hectic, and Leslie was out of her office much of the time. When she checked her voice mail at the end of the day, she had nothing from

Hampton. Either he hadn't gotten her message, or he was still out of town. Surely he would have returned her call had he known about it.

"You gonna leave your roses here over the weekend?" Sally called after her when Leslie walked past her desk at the end of the day.

"Why don't you take them?" Leslie suggested. "The way I've been sneezing today, I think I may be allergic to roses."

Sally shook her head. "No, thanks. But Mr. Meredith might enjoy them. You know, as a get well gesture."

"That's a good idea. I can drop them off tomorrow," Leslie said, wishing she had thought of it herself. "Write down his address for me, please."

Leslie was one of the last ones out of the building as she struggled to see around the masses of opening buds. Bracing the vase on the floor of the passenger's side, she opened the windows to the mild air. Although it was late September and the green mountains rimming the city had begun to hint of fall, the temperature remained pleasantly warm. Leslie still had not seen the city from the top of the mountain, and as she drove home, she made a mental note to do so soon.

Leslie was so engrossed with getting the roses up the stairs to her apartment that she didn't see the man standing near her door until she was almost upon him. She lowered the vase and saw a stocky, red-faced man in a three-piece suit regarding her without much expression.

"Miss Christopher? I hope I didn't startle you." The man briefly displayed a badge in a leather folder. "My name is Andrew Miller. I'm a special agent with the FBI. May I talk with you for a moment?"

"I suppose so," Leslie said, hoping there hadn't been some problem with her clearance.

"Those are nice roses," Mr. Miller said. "Did someone from Arrow send them?"

What an odd question! Leslie thought, a bit puzzled that an FBI agent would ask such a personal question. "No. They're just from a friend," she said, then sneezed.

"I see." Andrew Miller stood awkwardly in the middle of the room until Leslie motioned to an upholstered chair. She sat opposite him on the sofa.

"I hope there's no problem with my clearance. I understood that it had been approved."

"Quite true. I'm here on another matter." He looked at Leslie thoughtfully, then leaned forward slightly and lowered his voice. "Miss Christopher, for some time we have been concerned about a security leak at the ArrowSpace facility here in Huntsville. We've tried to find the source, but so far we haven't been able to get enough evidence to move in on anyone. We think you can help us."

"I don't understand."

"I can't give you the details, of course, but take it from me, there have been some pretty serious consequences as a result of the leaks at Arrow. Your background tells us that you are just the right person to help us find the guilty party—or parties, as the case may be—and that your own loyalty is beyond reproach."

He stopped for a moment as if waiting to see the effect his words would have. When Leslie said nothing, he continued in the same steady, measured tones, speaking softly as if he feared he might be overheard.

"We can do very little from the outside—there must be someone working on the inside. And with the VIRCO project coming up, you are ideally placed to help us. Will you do it, Miss Christopher?"

"Why me? I'm new to the Huntsville office and barely know my way around the building. I don't see how I could be at all useful."

"Actually, you're ideal for this assignment because you are new—and you don't have any contacts that are suspect. In addition, VIRCO is sensitive enough to attract attention from many different quarters. You must be aware that our country's defense could even be affected by this technology."

"Mr. Miller," Leslie said finally, "I understand there could be a serious security problem with this project, and certainly anyone who passes on information to unauthorized sources for any reason must be stopped. But why me? A dozen people have already begun work on the project, and every one of them has more experience than I do. Why not ask one of them?"

Mr. Miller leaned back and frowned impatiently. "I don't think you grasp the situation yet. We aren't sure where these leaks are coming from, so anyone at Arrow while the information was being passed on has to be suspect. That includes everyone in your office, from the chief down to the maintenance crew. But we can trust you, and we know you have the best chance to get evidence for us, if you are willing."

"Suppose I'm not? What happens then?"

Mr. Miller shrugged. "Either way you can keep on working as you are now. But keep this in mind—your VIRCO bid won't be worth a plug nickel to Arrow if another company steals its technology—and it could also cost our country a great deal if certain foreign powers got it. I don't think you'd want either result on your conscience."

"What would I have to do?" Leslie asked, and for the first time her visitor seemed to relax a little. *He thinks he's got me now,* she realized with a sinking feeling in the pit of her stomach.

"Not a great deal. From time to time you'll be asked to do certain things that might not make much sense to you, but could help us find the source of the security leak."

"Such as?" she asked.

He shook his head. "I can't give you the specifics now— it depends on how things seem to be going. We do have some contacts in place around Arrow—I'm sure you'll understand that I can't say who they are—and when they suggest things that might be useful for you to tell us, you'll be asked for the information. But, believe me, this won't interfere in any way with your regular job."

"There must be some strings attached. It can't be as easy as you make it out to be."

"Strings? I wouldn't say that, exactly, but there are a few conditions that we must insist upon. First, no one at Arrow is ever to know that you are cooperating with us. Not your boss or secretary or anyone else. Second, you are to contact me and only me if you come across anything we should know."

He handed Leslie a plain white card bearing a penciled telephone number. "I can be reached through this number, usually within a very short time. Don't hesitate to use it if you need it, but don't leave it lying around where other people might see it. And don't write it or my name down, either."

For the first time Leslie smiled faintly. *This whole thing is getting quite absurd,* she thought. Aloud she said, "I suppose I should memorize the number and then eat the card. Isn't that what spies do in the movies?"

Mr. Miller's face darkened, and Leslie realized that a sense of humor wasn't necessarily standard issue for FBI agents. "Miss Christopher, we consider this a serious matter," he said sternly.

"I'm sorry," Leslie said quickly. "How will you contact me?" she added, visions of all sorts of complicated plans coming to her mind.

"Usually by telephone, or I might drop by in the evening. However, I'll make sure you're alone first, so you won't have to deal with possible awkward introductions."

"You seem to have thought of everything," Leslie said, and Mr. Miller permitted himself a small smile.

"We try, Miss Christopher. Now, the first thing we need is a list of the names of everyone you hire to work on the VIRCO bid."

"Why?" Leslie asked, surprised.

"There are certain people who have been known to pass information from one company to another—nothing directly related to security as such, but certainly the kind of industrial espionage that Arrow doesn't want."

"I didn't know that," Leslie said and wondered if that was what Mr. Meredith's vague warnings had concerned.

"I know you didn't—that's why I'm here." Mr. Miller rose and walked to the door. "I'm looking forward to working with you, Miss Christopher."

"Goodbye, Mr. Miller." Leslie shook the hand he offered, then firmly closed the door behind him and leaned against it for a moment, considering what she had just done.

What have I gotten myself into? she thought, but Leslie

didn't see how she could very well have refused to coop-
erate. The more she turned over the interview in her mind,
the more confused she became. It was hard for Leslie to
think that anyone she had met could be a security risk,
but she had no doubt that the agent knew his business.

Now, she thought, *it's up to me to know my business as
thoroughly.*

∂

Leslie spent a restless night during which she dreamed
she went to work with a huge FBI badge on her blue suit
and was promptly fired. When she awoke on Saturday,
the agent's visit seemed remote and unreal. If it hadn't
happened, she wouldn't have to worry about it. In any
case, she reassured herself, nothing was likely to come of
it. Intrigue was entertaining in movies, but could it happen in the flesh, here in Alabama? Forget it!

As she sneezed her way through a late breakfast, Leslie
regretted leaving Hampton's roses in the kitchen. They
definitely had to go, and soon. After trimming the outer
petals, Leslie decided they still looked good enough to
take to Mr. Meredith. Leslie pulled on jeans and a pat-
terned cotton sweater and readied the roses for their last
ride. She decided against calling Mr. Meredith first; if he
was at home, she'd give him the roses. If he wasn't, she'd
get rid of them somewhere. Then she'd drive up the mountain.

The day was too nice to waste indoors. Sally had told
her that September and October were good months in
Alabama, and Leslie could see why. The air was cool and
crisp this morning, a welcome change from the oppres-
sive heat and humidity that had persisted in the first part
of the month, and everything seemed outlined in sharp

relief. Even the traffic moved along more smoothly than usual as Leslie negotiated the route to the older part of town where Mr. Meredith lived.

"It's a pinkish two-story house in the middle of the block," Sally had told Leslie. "Of course, it's way too big for him now, but after his wife died he said he'd keep it so his children would have a place to stay when they came to visit."

"Do you think he'll ever marry again?" Leslie had asked Sally, who responded with a shrug.

"Mr. Meredith doesn't seem to have much time for a personal life. He and his wife always lived quietly, and after she became ill, he devoted himself to her. It's been three years since she died, but he still seems to be grieving."

Leslie knew how that was. Her parents, who should have been enjoying retirement after years of constant traveling, had been killed by a drunk driver soon after Leslie had started to work in Los Angeles. Her life had gone on, though, and keeping busy had helped ease her pain. Apparently Mr. Meredith had gotten on with his life too. She gave him credit for keeping his personal problems to himself and suspected that he would prefer his employees to do likewise.

When she pulled her car into the driveway, Leslie noticed a couple of newspapers lying in the front yard, and as she approached the porch, she saw that the mailbox was jammed full. Leslie rang the doorbell and felt awkward when the door opened to reveal the usually well groomed Richard Meredith unshaven and wearing a wrinkled robe over his pajamas.

"I hope I'm not disturbing you," she said quickly. "I

have something for you out in the car. Are you all right?" she added, noting that he held onto the door frame as if to keep from falling.

"I've felt better, but I'm sure I need to be up and about more. Won't you come in?" he added, remembering his manners.

"Just for a minute—I'll be right back."

Leslie retrieved the flowers, noticing that they looked less lovely in the morning sunlight than they had under the artificial light in her kitchen. She set the vase on the front porch while gathering his mail and newspapers.

"I was just thinking I should bring those in," Mr. Meredith said when she handed the stack to him. Then he saw the vase and looked surprised. "Red roses! You must have some connections."

"Not really," Leslie said. She set the vase on a coffee table, the only surface in the living room that wasn't already cluttered. "I've enjoyed these for two days, and now it's your turn."

"Thank you for thinking of me. Please sit down."

"Is there anything I can do for you?" Leslie thought he looked quite ill, but he waved away her concern.

"I have a little stomach problem that acts up now and again. In a few days, I'll be good as new."

"We missed you yesterday," Leslie said. Her recital of some of the office "catastrophes" brought a faint smile to Mr. Meredith's pale face.

"Sounds like I picked a good time to stay home. What else has happened? Any luck with your staffing?"

"Some." Leslie wanted to tell Mr. Meredith about her visitor from the FBI, but since she had promised not to, she told him about the calls she had made. "I have some interviews lined up for early next week, so I hope to have names on those chart slots soon."

"Good," Mr. Meredith said. "Keep working on that lead computer scientist slot—that really is critical."

Leslie nodded. "I'd like to ask you about one of the consultants on the list. Do you know a Dr. Hampton Travis?"

Mr. Meredith looked at Leslie as if he thought she might be making a joke. "Certainly. Hampton Travis was one of the first non-pilot scientists to become an astronaut," he said.

"He was an *astronaut?*" Leslie said, tardily realizing why Hampton's name had seemed so familiar.

Mr. Meredith smiled faintly. "That was a long time ago," he said. "I take it that you have met the gentleman?"

Leslie nodded and felt chagrined at Mr. Meredith's knowing look. *What would he think if I told him the roses came from Hampton?* she asked herself, but she had no intention of telling him.

"Astronauts do seem to have a way with women," Mr. Meredith said dryly. "I don't suppose I need to remind you that mixing business and pleasure isn't a good idea, but Travis knows the ropes. When we get down to the wire on this proposal, that kind of experience can mean a great deal."

"Thanks for the information." Leslie stood. "Are you positive that I can't do something for you?"

"My housekeeper will be in later on today, and I'll be fine until then. But I do appreciate your concern—and if anything comes up at the office that you can't handle, call me. Maybe we can solve it together by telephone."

"Oh, don't worry about us. One way or another, we'll

manage to muddle through."

For the first time that day, Mr. Meredith smiled as if he really meant it. "That's what I fear the most!" he exclaimed as Leslie left.

He's a nice man, Leslie thought as she backed her car out of his driveway. She hoped she wouldn't disappoint him.

Before she started up the mountain, Leslie stopped to buy a sandwich and soda to take along. The main route up Monte Sano, known locally as Monte Sano Mountain, was a four-lane highway, but near the crest Leslie turned off onto a narrow, twisting road that straightened out as it reached the top of the mountain. She caught an occasional glimpse into the valley as she climbed higher, but trees hid most of the view. Leslie followed the signs to Monte Sano State Park, where Sally had said there were hiking trails.

When she reached the park picnic area, Leslie opened her trunk and took out her hiking boots. She had last worn them backpacking in Yosemite with the ArrowSpace/West Hiking Club. Those had been challenging mountains, and more than a thousand feet higher—not smooth and rounded like these at the southern end of the Appalachians.

Leslie looked around as she locked her car. In a meadow to her left was a small playground. Beyond it, a couple of teenage boys were throwing a Frisbee, which a wildly barking black dog kept trying to intercept. To the right and directly in front of her several families had gathered under the shade of the central pavilion. The smoke from hamburgers sizzling on the grill tantalized Leslie as she passed the picnickers and walked down the path to a bulletin board where hiking information was posted. From the several trails that began at that point, Leslie chose a two-mile walk which promised a waterfall and two over-looks in an easy loop.

A sign at the head of the trail gave the usual warnings about staying on the marked path, not disturbing any wild-life or vegetation, or climbing over the overlook fences . . . . Before starting on the hike, Leslie walked over to the bluff at the end of the picnic grounds and looked at the valley spread out below her, then down at the jagged rocks and underbrush on the other side of the low retaining wall. She recalled something Hampton had said about the moun-tain being dangerous. Certainly people who weren't watch-ing where they were going could lose their footing and fall, but it would be dangerous only to the careless.

Leslie turned into the woods and started down the trail, which was an almost too-easy walk. The promised water-fall was perhaps six feet high, hardly on a par with those in Yosemite. The overlooks offered views similar to the one she had seen at the edge of the picnic grounds, a check-erboard patchwork of fields and pastures bisected by streams and occasional swatches of woods.

After her hike, Leslie returned to the picnic area and sat on the low stone retaining wall. She pulled out the sandwich she had picked up at the deli and began her lunch. She felt a stab of loneliness that she had no one with whom to share the spectacular view.

Hampton Travis had offered to bring her up here, but she had refused his invitation, which hadn't been repeated. Then there was the matter of his roses—

"Nice, isn't it?"

The voice was so sudden and unexpected that Leslie gasped. For a second she had the crazy idea that thinking about Hampton had somehow caused him to materialize. But there he was, sitting down beside her on the ledge, his too-blue eyes regarding her steadily.

"You startled me."

"I'm sorry. I thought you saw me when you came out of the woods—you looked right at me."

"I guess I was thinking of something else."

"Deeply, no doubt."

"I got the roses. I was quite surprised," Leslie said.

"I thought you deserved them," Hampton said. "I know that a job like yours can be overwhelming, especially at first."

"It has been that, all right, but I'm holding my own."

"I never doubted you would."

"I tried to call you. You must be important, having an answering service."

Hampton shrugged. "Not really. I move around a lot, and I hate beepers and car phones and machines that try to talk like humans. The answering service comes in handy."

"Did they tell you I called?"

He looked amused. "They did, but I got in late last night, and you weren't at home this morning. I suppose you wanted to let me know you got the roses?"

"Yes, that was it," Leslie said quickly. She couldn't bring herself to tell him she had called to ask him to come in for an interview—in the light of what Mr. Meredith had said, it would effectively end any chance they might have for a more intimate relationship. She might have to do that yet, but on this beautiful day, Leslie wasn't ready to close that door.

"Looking at a view like this, it's easy to see why our

ancestors thought that God lived on top of a mountain,"
Hampton said, waving toward the valley below.

"They did?" Leslie said, then regretted it. Of course
she knew that the Greeks thought that the gods lived on
Mt. Olympus. *Hampton must think I'm hopeless*, she
thought.

He nodded. "'I will lift up mine eyes unto the hills,
from whence cometh my help,' the psalmist said. Of
course, we know that God is everywhere, but being on a
mountain always makes one feel closer to heaven."

"I suppose so," said Leslie, who had never thought about
it before.

"I was just about to have lunch—will you join me?"
Hampton waved to a picnic table under some pines, and
she walked over to it with him.

"They say great minds run in the same channels,"
Hampton said as he opened his backpack and brought out
a sandwich. "I see you stopped at the same deli. Do you
have Dijon mustard and bean sprouts too?"

"Of course."

"Is this the first time you've come up here?" he asked.

"Yes. I had no idea it was so lovely."

"If you like, I'll give you the grand tour—unless, of
course, you have other pressing business," he added, seeing her hesitation.

Leslie tried to think of a reason not to go with him but
could not. "All right," she said.

"Good—my car is over there by the field."

After they finished eating, Hampton took her to the top
of the mountain and another spectacular view. The southern part of the city stretched out before them, and Leslie
thought she could make out her apartment complex, or at

least part of it. With binoculars, she could probably see into her own living room—a thought that brought with it a mental note to make sure she closed her drapes, especially at night.

Hampton looked back out on the valley below them. "Can you find the Willows?"

"Not without binoculars," she said, noticing that Hampton had a pair slung around his neck.

Immediately he handed them to her. "Here, try these."

As Leslie attempted to focus the lenses, Hampton directed her movements with his hands covering hers. She was keenly aware of his nearness, of the spicy fragrance of his after-shave, of the electricity where their hands touched. After a few moments she lowered the glasses and glanced at the jumbled rocks just below. The touch of dizziness she felt wasn't entirely due to the height. When Leslie swayed a little and Hampton put an arm around her waist and drew her back, she quickly pulled away from him.

"We can't have you falling off the side of the mountain," he said.

Leslie returned the glasses and shuddered. "I have no desire to make the evening news that way, thank you."

"Feel like walking more? There are other trails nearby."

"I'm game. That first hike wasn't very much."

"This one is a bit steeper. The last time I took it I saw several deer."

"It's hard to believe we're so close to civilization up here," Leslie said after they had traveled several hundred feet on the trail. There was little underbrush in this area because the tall, canopied hardwood forest didn't admit enough light for anything to grow. From time to time they had to detour around a fallen tree or stump, and except for the occasional cry of a bird and the rustling of the trees' leaves in the pleasant breeze, the trail was silent and deserted.

Hampton took Leslie's hand when they climbed across a large tree limb in the path and continued to hold it as they walked.

"Is that a persimmon?" Leslie asked, pointing to a rough-barked tree.

Hampton shrugged. "I'm not sure. But for the record, if you ever get lost in the woods, don't walk to the left."

"Why not?"

"Lost people tend to do that—that's how they come to walk in circles."

"How interesting," Leslie said, her tone suggesting the opposite.

Hampton laughed. "I just wanted you to know that I'm not a total ignoramus concerning the woods."

Leslie looked levelly at Hampton and decided it was time to make him squirm a bit. "I know you're not an ignoramus, *Doctor* Travis. Why didn't you tell me who you were the first time we met?"

Hampton looked chagrined. "I suppose my ego was a little wounded that you didn't know. Anyway, all that astronaut business happened a long time ago."

"But it's an important part of your life, isn't it?"

Hampton nodded gravely. "Yes, it is. Once you've touched heaven, earth is never the same again."

Leslie shivered unaccountably. "I'd like to hear about it," she said.

"That can be arranged. Will you let me see you again?"

He had half turned to face her, his blue eyes regarding

her intently. As she looked into his eyes, Leslie felt her resistance draining away. She had worked hard all week. What harm could there be in getting to know an interesting person better? It had nothing to do with her work, nothing at all.

"I suppose so," she said at last. He nodded in satisfaction.

"You won't be sorry," he said. Hampton's expression brightened, and he pointed down the trail. "Come on. I want to show you a fossil bed just off the path over there."

Leslie followed him, trying to dismiss the nagging thought that by encouraging a personal association with Hampton Travis, she was, indeed, not only mixing business with pleasure but also somehow endangering her career and perhaps even the entire VIRCO project.

five

Hampton appeared promptly at seven, dressed in a navy blazer with matching slacks and a colorful paisley tie against his white shirt. She had chosen a full-skirted blue jersey dress, which she wore with a single strand of pearls and matching pearl earrings.

"Well, at least we're color-coordinated," Hampton said with a smile.

"Now will you tell me where we're going?" Leslie asked on the way to his car.

"Would it make any difference?" he asked. She shook her head.

"There must be two hundred restaurants in this town. So far I've been to about six, not counting the fast-food chains—I'm sure I've hit all of them."

"I doubt that you've been where we're going tonight," Hampton said.

Driving through the deepening twilight into the center of town, he stopped the car in front of an old building with a New Orleans-style courtyard, complete with old brick and elaborate wrought iron. They were greeted by a doorman, and a uniformed parking attendant drove the car away. At the entrance of the courtyard, a brass plate beside double doors read "Century Club - Members Only."

"Elegant," Leslie said, noting the circular stairway and crystal chandeliers in the marble-floored foyer. A young woman in black seated at a Louis XIV desk greeted

Hampton by name, then a maitre-d' in tails appeared from the dim recesses to the left and beckoned them to follow him.

After they were seated at a table for two in the rear of a small dining room, Leslie looked at the single yellow rose in a crystal vase, heard the muted notes of a piano playing in the main dining room, and realized that, whatever else the Century Club might be, it was not inexpensive.

"You're a member here?" she said, making it a question.

Hampton shrugged, a gesture she was coming to expect from him whenever he didn't particularly care for one of her questions.

"Yes and no. I did a favor for a member, a rather important old-cotton type, and he lets me use his membership on occasion."

"I'd think that 'on occasion' would be all one could afford," Leslie remarked, "or maybe once a year, on my salary."

"Good evening, sir, madam. May I bring you a cocktail?"

A white-gloved waiter clad in tails offered a tasseled, many-paged menu to Hampton, then a smaller one, lacking prices, to Leslie. *I wonder what they do when two women come in together?* Leslie thought, faintly annoyed at the assumption that a woman should automatically be sheltered from knowing how much a man was spending on her.

"How about it? Do you want something to drink before dinner?" Hampton asked, and Leslie shook her head.

"I don't drink," she said.

Hampton dismissed the waiter and turned back to Leslie

with a smile.

"Do you find it amusing that I don't drink?" Leslie asked somewhat defensively when the waiter left.

"Not at all. In fact, I had a hunch you didn't. It's always nice to know when I'm proven to be right."

Leslie looked closely at him, then took a sip of water from her glass. The moment she put it down, prepared to frame a reply, another waiter appeared from nowhere to refill it. Leslie could scarcely keep from laughing at the over-attentive service that persisted throughout the meal, making private conversation all but impossible.

When it seemed they might finally be left alone for a while, Hampton leaned forward and waved his hand in the direction of Leslie's head. "I like the way you've done your hair tonight."

Leslie had swept it back from her face into a French twist, hoping that it might give her a certain sophistication, but she was surprised that Hampton had commented on it. Most of the men she had known probably wouldn't have noticed her hair unless she dyed it purple or cut it into a Mohawk. "Thank you," she said. *Is he being sincere, or merely trying to flatter me?* Leslie privately wondered.

"I mean it," Hampton said, once more showing his uncanny knack of seeming to know what she was thinking. "I thought it needed to be said."

"You don't always say what needs to be said, though, do you?" Leslie countered.

Hampton cocked his head to one side and pursed his lips at her direct gaze. "That's a strange question. I wonder what's behind it?"

"Nothing sinister. I just don't quite know what to make

of you."

Hampton looked amused and cocked one eyebrow. "Oh?"

"You've learned a lot about me, yet I hardly know anything at all about you. And every time I ask where you're from or who you work for, it's like trying to grab a handful of fog."

"Apt phrase," he said with admiration. "However, you're wrong about me. I'm really quite substantial."

"You can't deny that you're not very forthcoming," Leslie persisted.

Hampton shook his head. "Let's just say that in my business, performance is all that matters. No one likes a blabbermouth."

"The Sphinx could be considered a blabbermouth compared to you," Leslie said, and once more Hampton smiled.

"You do have a way with words, Miss Christopher."

"Mine, perhaps, but not yours."

Hampton sighed. "All right, just what is so important for you to know?"

"For starters, let's talk about where you're from—and where you went earlier this week."

Hampton leaned back in his chair and looked reflective. "I'm really not from anywhere. My father was in the military and we lived all over the world. I never liked any of the places well enough to claim it as a hometown."

"I know how that is," Leslie said, thinking of her own childhood. "Didn't you feel that you were missing something?"

"Not really. People are more important than places, and my parents were careful to make sure that our quarters, however temporary, were a real home. "

Hampton broke off as one waiter appeared to remove their plates and another wheeled in a dessert cart.

"The Viennese torte is especially good tonight," the waiter offered.

Leslie shook her head. "I don't care for dessert," she said.

Hampton motioned for the waiter to remove the cart. "Just bring us coffee, please."

"Service is very good here," Leslie observed with a twinkle in her eye.

"Almost too good," Hampton said. Nothing further was said until their coffee had been served with elaborate ceremony and once more they were left alone.

"You were saying that you moved around a lot when you were growing up?" Hampton prompted, and Leslie shook her head.

"We were talking about you," she reminded him.

Hampton shook his head. "I'd rather talk about you. You must have had a very lonely childhood." He took her hand with such a look of compassion that Leslie realized she must have sounded more forlorn than she intended.

"My father kept thinking he'd find a pot of gold at the next job. I kept hoping he'd just stop somewhere long enough to put down roots, but he never did."

Leslie withdrew her hand and straightened in her chair. "That's all there is to my story—now it's your turn again."

The persistent waiter reappeared without warning. "Do you require anything further, sir and madame?"

"No, thank you. We'll be leaving now."

"Shall I have your car brought around?" the hostess asked when they reached the foyer.

"No, I think we'll take a turn around the park first, if

the lady here is willing."

Leslie glanced down at her high heeled shoes. "I certainly can't go very far or very fast in these, but if it's nearby, I'm game."

"It is. I'll be back for the car in half an hour," Hampton told the hostess.

As they went outside, Leslie noticed that the clock on the bank across the street indicated it was already past nine. "Is it safe to be out walking at this time of night?"

"We're practically next door to the police station, and everything is well lighted. See, the park is full of people," he added as they reached the end of the block and crossed the street to the Big Spring Park, built around the city's first source of water.

Several bicyclists and walkers passed them and they saw a family eating ice cream cones, despite the autumnal chill. Hampton took Leslie's arm as they walked around the little lagoon to sit in a gazebo where, Hampton said, there were summer concerts.

"You make a good tour guide," Leslie said.

"I'm good at a lot of things. You'd know that if you'd read my resumé."

"What makes you think I haven't?" she asked.

"Never mind—it doesn't matter."

"Oh?" *What happened to the man who wanted to work with me?* Leslie wondered. "Have you changed your mind about applying for the job?"

"It's still the greatest new program that's come down the pike since the Space Shuttle. But I didn't ask you out to talk about work."

Why did you ask me out, then? It would have been a natural question, but Leslie knew she shouldn't broach it.

"You never finished answering my question," she said instead.

"Which one?"

"About where you go when you leave town."

He gestured broadly with his hands. "Just about everywhere and anywhere. To Florida to see my folks, to Washington or L.A. or Houston on consulting jobs. Nothing exciting."

"Oh," Leslie said, somewhat deflated and annoyed. *What did you expect him to say?* she asked herself. He had told her what he wanted her to hear, but she doubted he'd told her the whole story. "I suppose nothing on earth could ever be as exciting as being an astronaut," she said.

Hampton glanced at Leslie, then pointed to the heavens, where a few stars shone above the city lights. "Exciting isn't the word," he said, then stopped as if trying to frame his words. "Have you ever experienced the feeling of weightlessness?" he asked.

"Not really. But I have done some scuba diving. Does that come close?"

"Yes, pretty much. In fact, astronauts train in the neutral buoyancy tank out at Marshall Space Flight Center— the first time I visited Huntsville, that was the reason. But there you always know that you're really in water. He pointed to the sky. "Up there, it's an entirely different sensation."

"The view must not be too shabby, either," Leslie said.

Hampton nodded enthusiastically. "You've seen pictures of our planet taken in orbit? Well, the stars are even more spectacular away from earth's atmosphere. Do you know the Eighth Psalm?"

"The only Psalm I know by number is the Twenty-third,"

Leslie admitted. "I didn't know any had to do with space."

"Actually, several do, more or less. The Eighth talks about how God set His glory in the heavens, and then the psalmist says, 'When I consider thy heavens, the work of thy fingers, the moon and the stars, which thou has ordained; What is man, that thou art mindful of him, and the son of man, that thou visitest him?' That's exactly the way I felt up there."

"I'm afraid I don't know much about the Bible." Even as she spoke, Leslie knew that she sounded defensive.

"Neither did I, until that first ride on the Shuttle. I can tell you, it made a believer of someone who'd seldom thought about God before."

In the darkness, Leslie couldn't see Hampton's face, but his voice rang with conviction. *If he's making this up, he should be an actor,* she thought. "That doesn't sound like what I'd expect to hear from a fact-and-figures computer genius," she said aloud.

Hampton chuckled. "Then you don't know many astronauts or what you call geniuses. The more we scientists learn about the complexity of the universe, the more respect we have for its Creator."

"Really?" Leslie asked, and Hampton again took her hand and held it loosely. She shivered, not entirely from the increasing night coolness. Hampton stood and helped her down the gazebo steps.

"Don't get me started on that topic," Hampton said. "We ought to go now—the car should be there by the time we get back to the Club."

They talked very little on the drive back to Leslie's apartment. He walked her to the front door. She didn't invite him to come inside, nor did he seem to expect that she would.

"Thank you for another lovely evening," she said.

"Likewise." Hampton brushed Leslie's cheek with the back of his hand, touched his forehead to hers, then pulled her to him and kissed her. Leslie made no effort to pull away, but neither did she allow herself to respond. It was almost as if her heart stopped beating for a moment, then resumed only when Hampton released her.

"You shouldn't have done that," she murmured, her voice so low that she wasn't certain that he'd hear her.

"I'll be in touch," Hampton said. He waited for Leslie to unlock her door and turn on an inside light before he touched his forehead in a farewell salute and walked away.

Sighing, Leslie double-locked the door behind him. Each time she saw Hampton Travis he intrigued her more, even though she felt that she knew even less about him. Whatever Hampton was—a God-fearing man genuinely interested in her, or an unscrupulous actor who would do anything to get on the VIRCO project—Leslie knew she ought to declare him off-limits. It was the only sensible course of action, given the circumstances. Yet Leslie wasn't prepared to shut out this man who interested her as no one else ever had.

I shouldn't make a hasty decision about him, she told herself.

❧

When she awoke Sunday morning, Leslie's first thoughts were of Hampton Travis and the pleasant time she always seemed to have in his company.

Does he go to church? she wondered, and tried to imagine which of the many houses of worship in Huntsville might attract him. For a moment she considered calling

Sally and inviting herself to Sally's church, but by the time she had finished breakfast she realized it was too late. Anyway, she had plenty of work to take care of that day.

As Leslie worked on VIRCO material on Sunday afternoon, she realized that she would need more help right away. The present Arrow staff had done a great job on the preliminary work, but they all had other duties too. With Mr. Meredith gone, Leslie was spreading herself pretty thin.

Whether or not she should work with Hampton Travis was becoming academic; VIRCO needed help, and he was certainly qualified. She'd be remiss in her duty if she let personal feelings interfere with considering hiring him.

Leslie went directly to Personnel as soon as she got to Arrow on Monday.

"I'd like resumés for these people," she said as she handed the desk clerk a brief list of names.

"We're shorthanded today. I don't know when I can get to them."

Leslie tried to sound pleasant but firm. "I really need these as soon as possible."

"So does everyone else," the clerk replied, but Leslie noticed that her request went to the top of the stack—a start, at least.

"Good morning," Sally greeted her a few minutes later. "Did you have a nice weekend?"

It was the sort of perfunctory question asked in all offices, and since Leslie had no intention of telling Sally about her date with Hampton Travis, she merely nodded.

"I took the roses to Mr. Meredith on Saturday. I didn't think he looked at all well."

"That's too bad. The work is piling up around here."

"I wish I had his clout in staffing," Leslie said. "Personnel's supposed to send up some resumés later—bring them to me right away, okay?"

Sally nodded and turned away to answer the telephone. Leslie went on to her office, where the faint aroma of roses still clung. She called down to Finance to check on the preliminary budget and had worked with the figures for a couple of hours when Sally brought in the requested folders.

"Here they are," she said, putting them on Leslie's desk. "Mr. Meredith's housekeeper just called to tell us he'll be out all this week, maybe longer. She's trying to convince him to go back to the doctor."

"He seemed to think he'd be all right in a few days. I hope this isn't anything serious."

"So do I, of course, but it doesn't sound good."

Sally left and Leslie rifled through the folders in search of Hampton's resumé. Twice she went through the stack, but it just wasn't there. With a sigh she dialed Personnel and told the clerk that at least one resumé she'd requested was missing.

"I'm sorry, Miss Christopher, but it's quite possible that some of them might be in another office. There are others hiring, you know," she added in a tone clearly meant to make Leslie feel that her request had been out of line. Leslie ignored the comment and asked the clerk to check and let her know who might have the folders.

"It won't do any good. Only one office works a resumé file at a time. If anyone else is considering the applicant, you'll just have to wait your turn."

"I see," Leslie said, forcing herself to sound more agreeable than she felt. "Can you let me know when the other resumés come back?"

"We don't usually do that."

"Is Mr. Birch in? I would like to speak to him about this."

"I'll transfer the call," the clerk said stiffly, and Leslie could imagine that her popularity with Personnel was about to hit the basement. She didn't care, though; she had a job to do, and Lowell Birch ought to know that his people were hindering it.

"Mr. Birch isn't in his office at the moment," his secretary told Leslie.

Leslie left her extension number and hung up, feeling frustrated. *A male program manager wouldn't get this kind of runaround,* she thought. She wished she could ask Mr. Meredith if Personnel were telling her the truth. She knew she had to play by the rules. But first she wanted to make sure that they were all using the same guidelines—and she was suspicious that they weren't.

"I'm sorry you're having problems, Miss Christopher," Lowell Birch said when he returned her call a few minutes later. He sounded at least a little sympathetic, which she took as a hopeful sign.

"So am I. I tried to find out who had the other resumés I need, but I was told that they had to be returned by the office who had them, presumably after they'd decided not to hire the people in question."

"Yes, that is the usual practice," Mr. Birch said, but something in the emphasis he put on the word "usual" gave her hope that he might be willing to bend the rules.

"Look, you know our situation with VIRCO," Leslie said earnestly. "If I can't get some people on board here pretty soon, there's a strong possibility that Arrow could miss the RFP deadline. Landing VIRCO would help Arrow's entire operation. I don't know what sort of priorities the other offices have, but it seems to me that at the least you can tell me now if anyone on my list is going to be hired for another project."

"Fair enough," Mr. Birch agreed. "I'll make a few calls and get back to you."

"Thanks—I really appreciate your help. And by the way, what's happening with the lead computer scientist slot? Have you heard anything else from the home office?"

"They've advertised the position. That's all I know."

"If there have been any responses, I'd like to have them right away," Leslie said.

There was a brief silence before Mr. Birch spoke again. "I understand that Mr. Meredith is on sick leave. The chief usually authorizes such activity. But you could prepare a FAX to be ready to go when Mr. Meredith signs the request."

"I'll do that right away. And in the meantime, I'd really like to get those missing resumés."

Leslie accepted Mr. Birch's assurances of cooperation, then thanked him and hung up, feeling somewhat better. Maybe it was just as well that Mr. Meredith hadn't been available, Leslie thought. He'd encouraged her to act on her own, and now that she was, Leslie was rather enjoying it.

Leslie's first victory turned out to be a small one, however. By the end of the morning Mr. Birch had located three of the four missing folders, but Hampton Travis's wasn't among them. No one seemed to be able to locate it, and of the others, two of the people had already been hired for other Arrow projects, and the other lacked the necessary experience.

"Sometimes I think everyone at Arrow is in a conspiracy against me," Leslie told Sally over lunch. "What did I do to deserve such hostility?"

"Some people around here are hostile to their own mothers. You just have to go on and do your best in spite of them."

"I know I wasn't Mr. Meredith's choice for this job. Maybe someone who wanted it resents me enough to make sure that things are going wrong for me."

"My, aren't we paranoid today!" Sally exclaimed. "To begin with, I doubt if anyone could mess things up more than Arrow's bureaucracy already does. That's really what you're up against just now. Anyway, the man who was most upset about not getting the job quit before you got here."

"Were all the other applicants men?"

"I have no idea, and we shouldn't even be talking about it. You're doing all right—I'll tell you if you happen to get off course."

Leslie smiled at Sally's declaration, but the information hadn't made Leslie feel any better. And when the rest of the day brought a breakdown in the mainframe computer and a temporary loss of data, Leslie felt even worse by the time she and Sally walked to the parking lot after work.

"This hasn't been one of my better days," Leslie said.

"What can you expect of Mondays? You need to take your mind off your troubles, and I know just the place. Come and ride with me—I'll bring you back to pick up your car later."

"You're not planning to take me to a singles bar, I hope," Leslie said.

Sally laughed. "No, that's not my scene. This is much better."

"I ought to do some work on the budget tonight," Leslie said.

"The budget can wait," Sally said firmly. "Your assistant says you need a break. Quit making excuses and come on."

"I hope there's food where you're taking me," Leslie said as Sally guided her car into the heavy traffic leaving the research park area. "That lunch salad didn't have much staying power."

"Oh, sure," Sally said. "Everywhere you look around here there's food. You ought to get your rose-giver to take you to some of them."

Leslie wanted to tell Sally that he had, but instead she shook her head. "I'm afraid I don't have the time or energy to worry about dating just now."

"More's the pity. But you know, a great social life isn't necessarily limited to one man. I called you Saturday to invite you to church with me on Sunday, but you were out. You really ought to try it, Leslie. Everyone needs a firm anchor—and working at Arrow has a way of making everyone need something to hold onto."

"I'm all right, thank you," Leslie said defensively. She wasn't sure what Sally meant about a firm anchor, but she wasn't interested in pursuing it. Then another thought came to her, and she looked at Sally feeling vaguely alarmed. "We're not going to your church now, are we?"

Sally laughed. "No, although some would probably say that this place is the most popular temple of worship in town."

Sally turned into the perimeter road around the mammoth shopping center that Leslie had noticed on her arrival in Huntsville, but which she hadn't visited.

"Don't tell me that your idea of fun is going shopping!" Leslie said accusingly when she realized that Sally was parking the car.

"Haven't you ever heard that when the going gets tough, the tough go shopping?" she teased. "No, of course I didn't bring you here to shop. Come on, you'll see," she added as Leslie still looked doubtful.

Leslie followed Sally into the main entrance of a mall that had a floor plan she'd seen a dozen times before. On two levels, the giant building was laid out like spokes in a wheel, so that from any point, one could see only a few of the more than two hundred stores. This particular evening, the first floor of the mall featured lavish displays from the area's many travel agents. Bright posters of far-away places vied for attention with hula-skirted girls and costumed couples performing national dances. A banner over the auditorium door announced that travel films were being shown continuously.

"This is a Travel Fair," Sally explained as they walked through the exhibits. "Maybe you read about it in the Sunday paper?"

"No, I didn't," Leslie replied.

"Well, this is your chance to get away from it all without taking leave or spending money," Sally said. "We can dine on Hawaiian or Mexican food, sample fresh pineapple, guava, and kiwi fruit, watch the dancers, and see all kinds of films. I come every year and enjoy it very much."

In spite of herself, Leslie found the Travel Fair to be entertaining enough to take her mind off her troubles for a few hours, and when they had seen all there was to see, she thanked Sally for bringing her.

"I told you you'd like it," Sally replied. "I have to make a quick stop at the Stocking Shop before we leave. Want to go with me?"

Leslie shook her head. "No, I'll wait here for you." She sat on a cushioned bench and looked around, content to watch the passing people and listen to snippets of conversation. A couple passed, arms around each other's waists, the woman's head resting on the man's shoulder. He bent down and said something that made her smile, and Leslie felt a small stirring of envy. A blue-eyed baby in a stroller stared at Leslie, then smiled and held out a balloon that bobbed in his chubby hand as he passed her. Leslie smiled back and waved at the child, who laughed in delight.

She was still half smiling when she saw the red-faced FBI agent walking toward her. He surely must have seen her—he looked directly at her—but Andrew Miller passed her without any sign of recognition. The same chill that Leslie had felt before in his presence prickled her skin. He hadn't contacted her since the night he'd asked her to help find security leaks at Arrow. She had half hoped that he'd forgotten about her and wouldn't ask her to do anything after all. But now that she had seen him again and he'd so pointedly ignored her, Leslie had an uneasy feeling that she might hear from him soon.

"Mission accomplished." Sally's voice startled Leslie. "Let's go—I still have one more surprise."

"I'm not sure I can stand anything else after all the excitement I've had tonight," Leslie said dryly. Sally laughed so heartily that several people turned to look at her.

"Oh, Leslie, maybe the Travel Fair wasn't all that thrilling, but at least it got you out of yourself for a little while, didn't it?"

"Yes, and I enjoyed it, but we should call it a day now."

"Almost. One more stop and we're done."

Sally was an aggressive driver, and Leslie didn't try to talk as she threaded the six-lane maze of traffic on University Drive and turned into the parking lot of an ice cream parlor.

"Here's the best-tasting treat in town," Sally said. "Let's see what the featured flavor is."

"I can't believe I'm doing this," Leslie said a few minutes later as they sat in Sally's car, holding double-dip cones of rocky road ice cream.

"Brings back my childhood," Sally said.

"Me too. Dad used to take me for ice cream as a special treat," Leslie said. "I don't think we ever had a refrigerator good enough to keep ice cream."

Sally launched into a rambling tale about her father, and as Leslie listened with amusement she idly glanced around and saw Hampton Travis enter the ice cream shop. Apparently he hadn't noticed her, and when he left the shop carrying two cones, Leslie turned her head back toward Sally and hoped that he wouldn't look their way. From the corner of her eye she saw him walk past a car to his Thunderbird. She turned around in time to see him hand one of the cones to a passenger in the front seat. In the brief light made when Hampton opened his door Leslie saw a dark-haired woman, but the distance between them was too great to make out the woman's features.

"What are you looking at?" Sally asked after she finished her story.

"I thought I recognized someone, but I was mistaken." Leslie glanced back in time to see the Thunderbird pull out into the road and meld into the traffic. "This has been fun," she said, wiping her sticky fingers with the thin paper napkin that had come with the cone. "Thanks for bringing me along."

"Hey, you're good company. And you'll still make it home by the ten o'clock news."

⁂

"Do you think she saw you?" Barbara asked as Hampton pulled away from the ice cream shop.

"Maybe." Hampton glanced at his rear view mirror several times, but the car in which Leslie had sat didn't appear. "I assumed they were going back to Arrow when they left the mall."

"I told you we shouldn't be out together."

Hampton grinned, but didn't divert his attention from driving. "Maybe Miss Christopher will be a little jealous."

"Don't joke about it, Hampton. This isn't very fair to her, you know."

"Let me be the judge of that. I have an idea that something will break soon."

"Don't you think she'll wonder what happened to your resumé?" Barbara asked, all business again. "The girl may be somewhat naive, but she isn't stupid."

"No, but she could be duped. The precautions I took earlier will come in handy. In the meantime, you know what you're to do."

Barbara nodded.

"I'll check with you at the usual time," Hampton added

as he stopped his car in front of Barbara's condominium.

He didn't offer to walk her to her door, and as the car pulled away from the curb, Barbara sighed. She and Hampton Travis had worked together before, and she knew he was very good at what he did. But never had she known him to become personally involved in a case. It was dangerous to allow feelings to interfere with work.

Men can be such blind idiots, even when they have a string of advanced degrees, she thought. She just hoped that Leslie Christopher appreciated him.

six

"Have you heard? Mr. Meredith is in the hospital," Sally greeted Leslie the next morning.

"No, I didn't know," Leslie replied. "Is it serious?"

Sally shrugged. "His housekeeper says he's gone in for tests and exploratory surgery, so maybe they'll find out what's wrong with him."

"I hope so," Leslie murmured.

"In the meantime, headquarters sent a FAX after we left yesterday about some applicants for the VIRCO positions, and there's also a lot of paperwork that needs Mr. Meredith's signature."

"I'll take them to him at the hospital—I need to talk to him, anyway," Leslie said.

Because of the two-hour time difference, it was too early for Leslie to call Arrow/West about the job applicants they'd located, but she added the FAX to the sheaf of papers in her briefcase. On her drive to the hospital, Leslie felt an unwelcome edge of frustration. The VIRCO project was supposed to be hers, yet everyone seemed to assume that she'd ask for Mr. Meredith's approval on all major decisions.

I really can do this on my own, Leslie tried to tell herself, but she was beginning to wonder.

Leslie finally located Mr. Meredith's private room in the maze of the hospital's corridors and was shocked to see how much worse Mr. Meredith looked than the last time she'd seen him.

"Well, this is a surprise!" he exclaimed when she entered the room. "I suppose my housekeeper must have called Arrow—I didn't want her to do that."

"You know how it is—we couldn't let you have a rest now, could we?" Leslie said lightly.

"I take it there's some business that can't wait," he said.

Leslie nodded. "Mostly just routine, but I also need your advice about staffing."

She opened her briefcase and handed Mr. Meredith the papers needing his signature. Despite his obvious discomfort, he scanned each one to make sure of its contents before signing it. Then Leslie gave him the FAX from headquarters. "Mr. Birch said you'd need to approve hiring any of these people."

Mr. Meredith looked at the names and nodded. "Pat Wentworth would be a valuable asset to this proposal—get him if you can. And Bob McLaren's a top-notch engineer, so you should make him an offer, too."

"Without a personal interview?" Leslie asked.

"I know the men, and they know what they'll have to do. Call them both today and ask if they can start right away. We're already too far behind in staffing."

Although his tone hadn't accused her, Leslie felt her cheeks warm. "I had a little trouble with some of the Personnel people, but they're cooperating with me now. I think I can wind up the other staffing quickly."

Mr. Meredith nodded. "Good." He gestured toward the hallway. "Close the door, please," he said.

When Leslie returned to his bed, Mr. Meredith handed her the sheaf of papers and waited for her to replace them in her briefcase before he spoke again. "If you hadn't come,

I was going to call you later today and remind you of the need for tight security at all points—files, trash, phone calls—the works."

"I hadn't forgotten," Leslie said.

"I hope not. You know that VIRCO is a prime target for all sorts of espionage."

"Yes, you told me that." *Something else must have happened,* she thought, and wondered if Andrew Miller had contacted Mr. Meredith.

"It's true. Internal security believes that a move will soon be made to obtain information on our proposal. In case anything suspicious comes up, there's an unlisted number that will directly connect you to the agent in charge of the case."

"Case," Leslie repeated, obviously surprised.

"Apparently someone is under suspicion, but the person who spoke to me couldn't—or wouldn't—tell me anything more. Of course, nothing may come of it," he added unconvincingly. "Give me a piece of paper."

Leslie opened her briefcase and detached one of her new business cards. With her pen, he scrawled a number she didn't recognize. It wasn't the same number Andrew Miller had given her—his was local, while this was an 800 number.

I wish I could tell Mr. Meredith that I already know about the investigation, Leslie thought, but Andrew Miller had been quite specific that she was not to tell anyone, including him. There was no doubt in her mind that Mr. Meredith wasn't involved in any way, but she had given the FBI agent her word, and there was no point in further upsetting a sick man, anyway.

Leslie talked briefly of other matters relating to the

office. Then seeing that Mr. Meredith was tiring, she rose to leave. "Let us know what the doctors find out," she said.

"I'm almost certain they're planning to carve me up like a Halloween pumpkin—they just haven't told me yet," he said.

Although he smiled, Leslie knew that Mr. Meredith couldn't be looking forward to the impending surgery.

"We'll take care of everything," Leslie said with slightly more confidence than she felt. "Try not to worry about Arrow."

"I won't. But in the meantime, you must promise to call me right away if you run into any trouble."

"Agreed," Leslie said, although she resolved it would take a major catastrophe before she would burden the ill man any further.

Back at Arrow, Leslie reported on Mr. Meredith, gave Sally the signed papers, then returned to her office with the folders that Personnel had just delivered. Quickly she looked through them, searching for Hampton Travis's. The file was suspiciously slender, and when Leslie opened it she saw why. The only thing it held was a note that the resumé had been withdrawn at the applicant's request.

Leslie closed her eyes and recalled how she had felt in his arms, and how much she had wanted to return his kiss. Instead, she had told him they couldn't see each other if they worked together. She had been right—just thinking about working with him made her heart race.

Opening her eyes, Leslie put the folder aside and tried to concentrate on the next one, but Hampton's blue eyes seemed to be mocking her as she did so.

Did he withdraw his application because of me? she

wondered. Or, more likely, she told herself, one of the consulting jobs he was always taking might be growing into a long-term assignment. *But why didn't he tell me he was doing this?*

"I'll just ask him." she said aloud, and rang his number before she could lose her nerve.

Once more a female voice answered, and in response to her query told Leslie that Dr. Travis had asked for his calls to be held until further notice.

"Did he go out of town again?" Leslie asked.

"I can't say," was the reply, and from her tone Leslie guessed that the answering service woman thought Leslie was probably some love-struck female, chasing a handsome man.

"Please have him call Leslie Christopher at Arrow when he checks in," she said, and hung up.

Leslie's hand was still on the receiver when her phone rang, and she took a deep, steadying breath before she answered it.

"I hope you plan to be at home this evening, Miss Christopher," a male voice said.

Although she had only spoken with him one other time, Leslie recognized Andrew Miller's voice and immediately tensed.

"Yes, I'll be home." Leslie wasn't surprised when he hung up without saying more.

What could he possibly want me to do? she wondered uneasily. *Something must have happened that I don't know about.*

Then the phone rang again, and for the rest of the day, Leslie had little time to speculate about anything other than her immediate duties. At least that way she didn't have time to worry about either Hampton Travis or the FBI agent—each disturbing in their own way.

❧

After Leslie had spent several restless hours wondering whether Andrew Miller would appear at all, he arrived just after nine o'clock.

"How is Mr. Meredith?" he asked when she admitted him.

"He's probably going to have surgery soon," she said.

"He'll be out of the office for some weeks, then, I expect." Andrew Miller began walking around her living room as if inspecting it for clues to some hidden crime, then he sat in a chair and motioned for Leslie to be seated, as well.

"The time has come for you to help us, Miss Christopher," he said. He was almost smiling, an expression that Leslie found even more sinister than his usual stern look. He leaned forward and dropped his voice as he had done before. "Here's what you must do. . ."

Later, when Leslie tried to reconstruct every detail of his visit, she recalled the way he had used the word "must." Not "Here is what we would like you to do. . ." Not "Here is what you can do to help us. . ." But "Here is what you *must* do."

He had told her she might be asked to do things that made no sense, and what Andrew Miller asked her to do certainly seemed to fit that category.

"Is that all?" she asked when he finished, and Andrew Miller permitted himself a half smile.

"For now. Just carry out my instructions and I'll be in touch later."

But how much later?

After the agent left, Leslie found herself recalling the warnings that both Hampton and Mr. Meredith had given her. "Be careful," each had said. To her knowledge, no one had appeared to be trying to steal information, but apparently someone might. And Leslie had been chosen to thwart it. It was a dubious honor, at best.

&

Leslie barely spoke to Sally when she walked past her desk the next morning and made an excuse not to go to lunch with her as they usually did. Never before had she violated even a single security procedure, much less walked out of a secure building with a briefcase full of confidential material. *I'll probably look so guilty I'll be stopped on general principles,* she thought.

But why should she worry if she were? After all, a breach of security would be handled by the FBI, and for all his lack of charm, Special Agent Miller would certainly vouch for her should the need arise. Still, as the day wore on, Leslie found herself dreading the time when she would have to carry out her orders.

"We got a lot done today," Sally said just before five o'clock. "I think we've earned an evening out—dinner and a movie, maybe. How about it?"

"It sounds tempting," Leslie replied truthfully. "But I still have some work to do."

"I'll stay and help. Many hands make light work, as they say."

"Thanks, Sally. I appreciate the offer. But this is something I must do myself."

"Are you sure?" Doubt was written on Sally's face. "I'll wait for you if I can't help. . ."

"No, no," Leslie cut in, too abruptly, she realized. The

last thing she wanted was to make Sally suspicious. "It may take a while. I'll take a rain check, all right?"

"Sure, but remember—Arrow managers don't get a dime of overtime."

Leslie stayed at her computer terminal for at least fifteen minutes after the last employee departed, then she tried to print out the data she had on VIRCO. When the printer refused to respond, Leslie realized that the sensitive documents couldn't be printed without special bypass procedures. And the instructions for those procedures were locked in the vault adjacent to Mr. Meredith's office.

Leslie moved cautiously into the corridor, acutely aware of the clicking sound of her heels on the polished tiles. She made sure that no one was around to see her enter his office or go to the safe-like door that guarded many Arrow secrets. Leslie closed and locked the office door behind her and approached the vault on tiptoe, even though the carpeted floor muffled her steps. She swallowed hard, then put a tentative hand out to the dial. Mr. Meredith had told her the combination as soon as she had her clearance and made sure that she could open the vault, close it, and then open it again. He hadn't had to tell her not to write down the combination; she already knew that. But she hadn't worked it since, and Leslie feared that she might not be able to open it on her first try.

"This vault is like an automated bank teller," Mr. Meredith had told her then. "It'll allow you to try to open it twice. The third time, if you still don't have the right numbers, an alarm goes off in Security. They don't like for that to happen."

Neither would I, Leslie thought as she twisted the fat

metal dial. There were five numbers in the sequence, re-set periodically. She didn't think the combination had been changed since Mr. Meredith had gone on sick leave. She would have been told if it had been.

Or would she? Leslie felt perspiration gathering around her forehead and beading on her upper lip as she put in the last number, pulled the handle—and nothing happened. She thought she recalled the numbers, which she had memorized by using the first part of the street number of her Los Angeles apartment. Maybe she had just gone past one or more of them.

Once more Leslie tried, so deliberately that she was certain she had hit each number exactly. But as before, the handle didn't yield. Leslie closed her eyes and tried to visualize Mr. Meredith as he had opened the combination. She was almost positive she had the right numbers; maybe she hadn't cleared the combination properly.

Taking a deep breath, Leslie whirled the dial to the left to clear the combination, then to the right for the first number; further right for the next one; past zero to the left for the third; back to the right for the fourth; and to zero again as the last number. She thought she'd done it perfectly, but at first it seemed the vault wouldn't open that time, either. Leslie was trying to think of a good reason to be found trying to open the vault after hours, anticipating the alarm that was about to sound in Security, when she heard a soft "click," and the handle turned. Quickly she opened the door and began to search for the manual she would need to override her computer.

"Of course it would be in the last place I looked," she muttered. Not daring to remove the manual from the vault, Leslie scanned its pages until she found what she needed, then carefully replaced the book in the file, closed the vault door, and twisted the dial one last time.

Again the corridors were empty as Leslie returned to her office and fed the required information to her computer. A few beeps later, the printer responded to her command, and page after page of flow charts and drawings began to print out. At one point she had to stop the process to add more paper, but finally all the information was printed, and with a last double beep, the printer turned itself off. Leslie gathered up the sheets, without bothering to remove the edges. A glance at her watch showed that it was already seven o'clock. Hurriedly she stuffed the printout into her briefcase, only to find that she had to remove the other papers before it would fit. Then she locked the briefcase. Leslie knew that Arrow Security guards sometimes asked workers to open their cases, but often waved them on if the cases were locked. It didn't make a great deal of sense to Leslie, but then, many things at Arrow seemed illogical.

Leslie looked around her office one last time to make sure she hadn't left anything incriminating. She walked out to the elevator, intensely aware of the rapid beating of her heart. As the elevator descended smoothly to the ground floor, she decided she must lack some character trait that would allow her to enjoy subterfuge and intrigue. *Some people must like it,* she thought as she walked toward the Security station near the front entrance. *Otherwise, where would all the spies come from?*

"Good night," Leslie said to the guard. An older man who looked as if his feet hurt nodded curtly and held the door open for her. Then she was outside, walking down the familiar path in the fall twilight, feeling exactly as she had when she was twelve years old and some kids she had wanted to make friends with had dared her to take something from the corner convenience store. As long as she lived, Leslie would remember how she felt walking out of the store, a candy bar she hadn't paid for heavy in her coat pocket. She hadn't been caught, but the next day she went back and paid for the candy bar, and never again had she tried to make friends that way. She and her parents had moved on soon after, and Leslie had almost forgotten the incident.

Leslie put the briefcase in her trunk, something she rarely did, and drove home carefully, trying not to call attention to herself by breaking any traffic laws. She remembered cases in which a criminal had successfully eluded the police, only to be stopped for some minor driving infraction and thus had been captured. She pictured herself in jail, then scolded herself for allowing such thoughts. After all, she was working on the right side of the law, even though appearances might indicate the opposite.

As Leslie retrieved her briefcase, a couple who lived near her in the same building pulled up beside her car, and they exchanged greetings.

"Don't you know better than to bring work home?" the man asked.

"This may look like a briefcase, but it's really my lunch box," Leslie said.

"It certainly beats brown bagging," the woman said with a chuckle.

Leslie's smile faded rapidly as she let herself into her apartment. She wanted to sit in the dark and not answer the door or telephone. She wanted to be in Los Angeles, among people she knew and trusted. She wanted to be anywhere else, doing anything other than sitting here in her apartment, waiting for an FBI agent.

Leslie changed into jeans and a soft sweater. Feeling a faint stirring of hunger, she cooked a frozen entree in her microwave. As she ate, she thought of the contrast between this, her usual evening meal, and the sumptuous feasts Hampton Travis had lavished upon her.

I shouldn't be thinking of him at a time like this, Leslie told herself. *Or, for that matter, at any time.* He obviously didn't want to work with her, after all. Or maybe he had gotten a permanent assignment elsewhere and hadn't bothered to tell her. He certainly hadn't bothered to tell her about the brunette—why would he tell her about a change in career plans? The man was illusive, that much she knew. At least Leslie had her work to divert her thoughts.

Leslie sighed and reluctantly turned her attention to her assignment. She unlocked her briefcase and removed the papers she'd smuggled out of Arrow. Laying them out on the sofa, she began separating the printout by categories—the time lines, organization charts, preliminary sketches, technical drawings, budget figures—a dozen parts of the preliminary RFP gathered in one place for the first time in its short history. *Gathered illegally,* Leslie thought sourly, but then she reminded herself that anything for the FBI couldn't be illegal.

Leslie was still separating the pages when the doorbell rang. Making no effort to conceal the papers, Leslie opened the door without looking through the peephole first.

"Hello—I was hoping I'd catch you at home. Do you have a minute?"

Leslie's mouth fell open in astonishment as Hampton

Travis, apparently taking her silence as consent, walked into her apartment—and headed straight for the sofa and the VIRCO papers.

seven

This isn't happening, Leslie tried to tell herself, but she knew quite well that it was.

"What do you think you're doing?" she asked when she could speak again, although it was obvious that he was looking at the VIRCO papers.

"I'm wondering the same thing about you," Hampton said, strangely formal. "I think we need to have a talk."

"Not now—I'm expecting someone." Leslie walked to the sofa and stood in front of it as if to bar him from seeing any more.

"This won't take long. In fact—"

Hampton broke off as the doorbell rang.

Andrew Miller, Leslie thought immediately. *He mustn't find Hampton here or know that he saw the papers.*

"I presume that is your guest?"

"Yes." Leslie glanced nervously at the door. "It would be best if he didn't see you here."

"Oh?"

Leslie felt her cheeks warm as Hampton raised his eyebrows in a knowing look. Helpless to correct his impression, Leslie steered Hampton into the kitchen. "You can go out the back door," she said as the doorbell rang again.

"Why do I get the feeling that I'm being thrown out?" he asked as Leslie opened the door and all but pushed him through it.

"Probably because you are. I'm really sorry."

"Maybe I should come back when you're not so busy," he said, but Leslie had already closed the door.

Feeling as if she had weights on her feet, Leslie crossed the living room and admitted Andrew Miller. His sharp glance swept around the apartment before he spoke.

"Are you alone?" he asked. Leslie nodded and vaguely wondered what the penalties for failure to make a full disclosure to a federal agent were.

"It took you long enough to come to the door. Is this all the VIRCO material?" he added when Leslie offered no excuse for her delay in admitting him.

"Yes, all we have so far." Leslie watched as he rifled through the printout.

"No one saw you take them out?" At her nod, he added a muttered, "Good work."

"I still don't know why I had to do this," Leslie said, but the agent was seized with a sudden fit of coughing and did not reply. She watched as he began to examine each of the pages. "Wouldn't it be easier to take the whole printout? I certainly can't keep it around here."

Taking another coughing fit, Miller couldn't speak for a while. Finally he said, "Your computer system knows that classified information has been printed out, and it must be accounted for. Log the printout into the vault until it's time for the next step."

"What next step?" Leslie asked, alarmed that he intended to ask her to do more.

In reply, Miller bent in a convulsion of coughing that made his face even ruddier.

"Are you all right?" Leslie asked as the paroxysm showed no sign of ending.

He pulled out a handkerchief and wiped his brow. "A

sip of water might help," he managed to say between more coughs.

"I'll get it right away," Leslie said.

When she returned, Mr. Miller drank the offered glass of water at a single gulp.

"Thank you, Miss Christopher. That helped."

"I believe you were saying something about a next step?"

"Yes. You know our purpose is to find the person responsible for Arrow's security leaks. So far you have very little that would be of value to another company. When will you have more technical figures?"

"I'm not sure," Leslie replied, although she had asked the engineers to submit their preliminary work no later than the following Friday. "Our lead scientists aren't in place yet."

"Then you really are behind," Mr. Miller said.

Once more Leslie tried not to sound defensive. "A little, but we'll move much faster when the whole group gets together."

Mr. Miller looked pleased. "Then we'll see who takes the bait."

"What bait?" Leslie asked, not liking the sound of it.

"Just a manner of speaking, Miss Christopher. Your cooperation today indicates that you can be trusted, and for that we thank you. I'll be in touch."

Andrew Miller hadn't been in her apartment for more than a few minutes, but as Leslie closed the door behind him, she felt that she'd aged at least a year. Now that he was out of the way, she returned her attention to Hampton Travis. *He'll think I'm carrying on a hot romance, shoving him out like that,* she thought with a glint of a smile. Then she wondered why he'd showed up, at night and unannounced, in the first place. Why hadn't he returned her phone call? Furthermore, he'd seen the VIRCO material—certainly not enough to get any detailed information, but close enough to know what it was.

Leslie had just started to put the papers back together when an insistent knock sounded at the back door. Leaving the papers as they were, she let Hampton in.

"Is the coast clear now?" he asked.

"My visitor is gone, as I'm sure you know. What did you do, hide in the shrubs and watch us through your binoculars?"

"That wasn't necessary," he replied. "I don't know why you're so upset—I'm the one who got thrown out."

"I'm sorry. Come in." Deliberately Leslie stacked the VIRCO papers on one end of the sofa, face down. "If I was rude, I'm sorry. This hasn't been a very good day."

"Apology accepted. Now let's start over, shall we?"

"At what point?" Feeling the need to put more distance between them, Leslie took a step backward.

"At the point where I told you you shouldn't have brought those papers home," he said.

"You shouldn't have looked," she said.

Hampton reached for the top page, a staffing flow chart, and the whole stack slid to the floor.

"Wonderful," Leslie muttered. She lunged at the pages, which were quickly scattering over the floor, and made an effort to pick up as many as she could. The papers were now completely out of order, but she didn't care.

"I asked who your visitor was," Hampton said as he bent to retrieve more pages. "If you don't want to tell me, that's your business. But I don't want to see you get hurt."

Leslie felt her face warming again at the implied

criticism in Hampton's tone. "I don't intend to. Believe me, this has nothing to do with you. And while we're asking questions, you might tell me why you withdrew your resumé."

It was Hampton's turn to look surprised. "You mean you finally got around to considering me for a job?"

"You said you were qualified," Leslie said somewhat stiffly. "I would have considered you for the lead computer robotics slot."

Hampton's eyes twinkled. "That's mighty generous of you, Miss Christopher. Maybe I should've kept myself in the running, after all."

Leslie dared to look him in the eye. "Why didn't you?"

His expression now serious, Hampton returned her gaze. "Be honest—would you really have hired me?"

"I don't know. I suppose it would depend on whether your resumé showed that you were qualified."

"Oh, I'm qualified, all right. In fact—well, never mind that. The question is, would you continue seeing me if we were working together?"

Leslie looked away, afraid of what her eyes might be tell him. "If we worked together, I'd see you every day, like it or not."

"You know that's not what I mean." Lifting her face with a hand under her chin, Hampton forced her to look at him. "Would you go out with one of your employees socially?"

Leslie shook her head. "No."

"That's what I thought."

Hampton put his arms around Leslie and drew her to him so quickly that, even if she'd wanted to, she had no chance to protest.

"You hardly know me—and I know even less about you," Leslie said.

Hampton pulled back to look at her, then embraced her again. "I know this much," he said just before his lips met hers.

"Oh, Hampton—" Leslie began, but before she could finish, he kissed her again. This time she responded willingly.

"Maybe I should have taken the job to keep an eye on you," Hampton said when he finally released her. "You don't seem to have any idea that you might be in danger."

Leslie's look of surprise was genuine. "I certainly don't," she agreed.

"Then it's time you did. If you ever need help, I hope you'll let me know."

Seeking to lighten the atmosphere between them, Leslie smiled. "If I have to wait for your answering service to find you, I'd probably already be done in," she said somewhat tartly.

Hampton had continued holding Leslie, but now he released her and removed a slip of paper from the breast pocket of his jacket. "This is a private number where I can be reached. Use it if the need arises. I have to go now."

Leslie put the paper in her jeans pocket without looking at it and followed Hampton to the front door. "Does that mean you're going to stay in town for a while?" she asked.

Hampton put out his hand to touch her cheek, then traced the line of her eyebrows with his thumb and touched the tip of her nose. "I'd like nothing better, but the people I did my last consult for want a few changes in the final design, and it can't be done long distance. I may be around here a few more days, then you can be sure I'll get back as soon as I can."

"I hope so," Leslie found herself admitting as he pulled her into his arms for a kiss that left her breathless.

"Don't forget to use your deadbolt lock," Hampton said. Then he was gone.

Hampton seems obsessed about my safety, she thought as she double-locked the door. Compared to Los Angeles, Huntsville was a relatively crime-free haven. However, she was beginning to realize that there might be other hazards here that she hadn't even considered.

It's nothing to worry about, Leslie told herself. With one last look at the VIRCO papers, she turned off the living room lights and left the room.

❧

The next morning Leslie felt a little ridiculous as she walked past the security guard, the VIRCO printout safely locked in her briefcase. She chided herself for having been so paranoid the night before. In the light of day, the whole business seemed absurd, much ado about what had turned out to be very little—and she hoped it would stay that way.

When Leslie reached her office, she dumped the printout on her desk and began to put the pages back in order. Now that she had it, she thought she might as well use it, especially since, as Mr. Miller had pointed out, the internal security system would alert Security that it had been printed.

"Hi," Sally said from the doorway. "You're up and at 'em pretty early this morning, aren't you?"

"Or maybe you're late. I'm trying to see the big pic-

ture—this is a printout of our work so far," she added as
Sally cast a quizzical look at the pile of papers on Leslie's
desk.

"It looks like a pretty good jigsaw puzzle. Did you log
it in with Security? I'm not sure anyone told you needed
to do that."

"They didn't," Leslie said, and wondered what else an
ill Mr. Meredith might have overlooked telling her or assumed she already knew.

"Then I predict you'll hear from Security shortly. If they
complain, you can always plead ignorance."

Leslie smiled. "I could plead that to a lot of things,"
she replied.

"Don't forget that Pat Wentworth and Bob McLaren
are processing in today," Sally added from the door.

"Great—I'll feel much better when I know they're working on this."

But as soon as Sally left, Leslie returned to sorting the
papers, wondering why Mr. Miller hadn't warned her to
notify Security in the first place. Surely he knew Arrow's
procedures. And why did she have to bring it home? Nothing about the whole thing made any sense to her.

Then another problem presented itself as she completed
sorting and counting the papers—she was one short.

I must have missed a page somewhere, she thought,
and counted again. But this time there was no question
about it—the page that held the only really critical data
she had gathered so far just wasn't there anymore.

Leslie looked in her briefcase and under her desk. She
even lifted her desk blotter, but to no avail—the budget
page was missing. She thought back to the night before,
when both the FBI agent and Hampton had seen the print-

out. Only Mr. Miller had handled the pages—except, she recalled, when Hampton helped her pick them up after she dropped them. Could he have taken the budget page at that time? Leslie thought it wasn't likely.

It's probably under the sofa, she told herself and wished she could go back to her apartment and look for it that very moment. Since she couldn't, Leslie bundled up the printout and locked it in her filing cabinet, awaiting the arrival of Pat Wentworth, who would need to see part of it. She had just slipped her key ring into her purse when Sally rang her.

"A visitor from Internal Security is on the way to your office now," she warned.

"Thanks," Leslie replied, replacing the receiver as some-one rapped lightly on her door. "Come in," she invited, and a young woman in a very red dress entered the office. Leslie noted that her visitor was tall, attractive, brunette—and familiar.

And every single time she had seen her, the woman had been with Hampton Travis.

"Miss Christopher?" she was saying pleasantly, her hand extended for a firm handshake. "I'm Barbara Redmond, from Internal Security."

"Is there a problem?" Leslie asked, deciding that igno-rance would be her best defense.

"In a way. It seems that you printed out some sensitive material without first notifying us."

"I didn't know I should," Leslie replied, honestly enough.

"Well, now you do. Here are the proper forms to use the next time you want a printout from the Arrow mainframe. And here's the one to sign today."

Leslie glanced at the heading on the second page and frowned. "This is a Report of Security Violation. Can't I just postdate one of these other forms?"

"I'm afraid that's against the rules. Don't let the title bother you, though—it's really pretty routine."

"Security violations are routine?" Although the woman had made every effort not to appear intimidating or sound threatening, Leslie felt that Security had taken her measure and found her short of the mark.

"Of course not. I can also assure you that this won't affect your job performance rating, Miss Christopher. You're new, and if no one explained our procedures, you certainly can't be blamed for not following them."

"It won't happen again. What else should I know that I don't?"

Barbara Redmond looked directly at Leslie. "Most of our security rules are common sense—probably the same ones you had in Los Angeles, except for our extra computer precautions. And you don't, of course, ever leave the building with classified information."

Barbara Redmond's words made Leslie flush guiltily. Her instincts had been correct—she shouldn't have removed the documents. And she wouldn't have, if the FBI agent hadn't practically ordered her to do so. But Leslie couldn't say so without breaking her vow to remain silent. *Maybe this is part of my test,* she thought.

"I've heard that Arrow has some problems with industrial espionage. Do these rules have anything to do with that?" Leslie asked.

"Our security regulations are standard with the aerospace industry," Barbara replied, pointedly evading Leslie's question.

Leslie's intercom buzzed, and Sally announced that Dr. Wentworth had arrived.

"Thank you. Tell him to wait, will you?"

Barbara Redmond stood. "I won't take any more of your time, Miss Christopher. Don't forget to sign that form and send it to me as soon as you can."

She already had her hand on the door when Leslie called to her to wait.

"One more thing—I believe you know a man named Hampton Travis. He had applied to work on VIRCO, but apparently he's changed his mind."

Barbara's expression didn't change, but the way she looked away made Leslie believe there could have been— and might still be—something personal between them. "I haven't seen Dr. Travis lately. I didn't know he'd given up on VIRCO," she said

I'm sure you didn't, Leslie thought, not believing a word. Maybe Leslie hadn't figured out exactly what was going on, but there was no doubt in her mind that Barbara Redmond knew a lot more about Hampton Travis than she was about to tell her.

"Good luck with your project," Barbara said in parting.

"And the same to you with security," Leslie rejoined, letting Barbara make of it what she would.

Leslie knew that even though she could try to put them all—Barbara Redmond and Hampton Travis and Andrew Miller—out of her thoughts, they'd all soon be back.

One thing was certain—Leslie devoutly hoped that Andrew Miller wouldn't expect her to violate security again.

❧

Back in her first floor office, Barbara Redmond reached

for the telephone and leaned forward, speaking quietly when Hampton answered.

"We must talk," she said without any preliminaries.

"How soon?"

"After work today will do—about six o'clock, my place?"

"I'll be there."

Barbara hung up the telephone and deliberated whether she should cook for him. It'd be safer than going out to eat, she told herself. Already, too many people had seen them together.

And it was always pleasant to spend time with Dr. Hampton Travis.

⁂

Leslie quickly briefed Pat Wentworth and Bob McLaren, who arrived at almost the same time. She was immensely relieved when they both seemed to know what needed to be done. While she was talking to them, Lowell Birch called to tell her about a retired military officer with many years of experience dealing with complicated systems. VIRCO would need someone with both experience and maturity as they raced to complete their preliminary proposal, and Leslie told him to ask the man to come in to see her as soon as possible.

"I can't believe that Dr. Wentworth is such a hunk," Sally told Leslie when the men left to check in with Personnel. "I was expecting a real computer nerd."

"So much for stereotypes." Leslie smiled, thinking that Hampton Travis was another good example of the folly of pre-judging people—by their occupations or anything else. "For your information, he's also a widower, no children...."

"Be still, my heart!" Sally exclaimed dramatically.

"Try not to distract the man too much, at least not before we get this proposal finished."

Sally put on an exaggerated look of one wrongly accused. "You know nothing will keep me from helping you get VIRCO ready. But after hours, he's fair game."

Leslie chuckled, but as she walked back to her office she wondered why she hadn't found Pat Wentworth as attractive as Sally had—in fact, she'd hardly taken notice of his looks at all. Perhaps it was because she'd been more concerned with his academic and scientific credentials to notice. Or maybe it was because something—or someone—else had kept Leslie from thinking of him personally, knowing they'd be working closely together.

I won't make the same mistake twice, she told herself, although she still wasn't sure how she could have done anything differently with Hampton.

Hastily eating a sandwich at her desk, Leslie tried to call Mr. Meredith to tell him she had filled all the key positions, only to be told that he'd already been taken from his room to be prepped for surgery.

"I just found out that Mr. Meredith's going to be operated on this afternoon. I'm going to try to see him if I can—I know he's been concerned about the VIRCO staffing, and maybe knowing it's going well will make him feel better," Leslie told Sally a few minutes later.

Sally looked concerned. "I thought he'd let us know when the surgery was scheduled. I'm glad you're going. Tell him I'm saying a prayer for him."

On her way down in the elevator, Leslie thought of Sally's words. She would pray for him, Sally had said, and Leslie had no reason to doubt it. There was a bond between all people who shared a belief in the power of prayer, and for a moment Leslie felt a sense of loss that she wasn't a part of that close fellowship.

I suppose I can pray for him in my own way. On the drive to the hospital, Leslie did just that, and hoped that her awkward efforts had been heard.

The information desk clerk directed Leslie to the Surgical Waiting Room, where she was told that she was too late to see Mr. Meredith. "He's already in surgery. You're welcome to wait with those people over there if you like."

Leslie looked in the direction the clerk indicated and saw half a dozen people sitting off to one corner of the large waiting area, including a young woman she supposed to be Mr. Meredith's daughter and a middle-aged woman whom she guessed was his housekeeper.

Thanking the clerk, Leslie joined the group. "I'm Leslie Christopher—I work for Mr. Meredith at Arrow. We didn't know he was going to be operated on so soon."

"Hello, Miss Christopher—I'm Alicia Meredith. We didn't know either—the doctors just got some results back and decided they should operate right away."

"I'm glad you could come, Miss Meredith—I'm Mary Gardiner, Mr. Meredith's housekeeper. He's been real worried about y'all at work."

"I know," Leslie said. "I thought it might make him feel better to know that things are going really well now."

A tall man with silvery white hair smiled and extended his hand to Leslie. "I'm Paul Carew, his pastor. It's good of you to come to the hospital, as busy as I know you must be."

"I wanted to offer what support I could," Leslie said.

Pastor Carew introduced Leslie to his wife and another couple from the church. "We were just about to have prayer.

Will you join us?" he asked.

Leslie nodded. Everyone stood, forming a loose circle. Alicia Meredith on her right and the pastor's wife on her left reached out to hold Leslie's hands. All bowed their heads as Paul Carew began to pray, speaking softly and earnestly.

Why, he's talking to God as if He were right here with us, Leslie thought with wonder, expecting the pastor's prayer to be more flowery. She'd seldom seen people praying outside of a church, although she'd once had a friend whose family always joined hands around the table for grace before meals.

"Amen," the pastor concluded, and some of the others added their own "amens."

"Will you wait with us, Miss Christopher?" Alicia Meredith asked.

"How long will the surgery take?" Leslie asked.

"The doctor didn't say—just that it depends on what they find when they get started. It could be several hours."

"I'm afraid I have to get back to work," Leslie said regretfully. To her surprise, she found herself wishing that she could stay there and get to know Mr. Meredith's attractive young daughter and experience more of the calming effect the small group seemed to have on her.

"We understand. I'll tell Daddy you were here," Alicia said.

"I understand you're new in town, Miss Christopher," Paul Carew said. "We'd be glad to have you visit our church, if you haven't found one here yet."

"Thank you—I'm afraid I've been too busy to do much on weekends," Leslie said.

"Don't put it off—you're missing a great blessing," the

pastor's wife said in parting.

On her way back to Arrow, Leslie wondered what it'd be like to be part of a close-knit group like those church members who had gathered to pray for Mr. Meredith. *Maybe I should have taken Sally up on her invitation,* she thought.

But for the time being, Leslie had other things on her mind—like the whereabouts of the missing printout page. Even the news, several hours later, that Mr. Meredith had come through complicated stomach surgery in good condition only lifted her spirits temporarily.

"I suppose your prayers worked," Leslie said to Sally after hearing the news.

"Prayer always does," Sally replied.

Maybe I should ask for divine assistance in finding that pesky missing page, Leslie thought, but she was sure that God didn't care about petty problems like hers.

eight

When she reached her apartment in the semidarkness of the early November evening, Leslie pulled the drapes, turned on every light in the living room, and began to search for the missing budget page. She got down on her hands and knees to look under the sofa. Then she moved the drapes aside, picked up every chair and sofa cushion, and emptied the wastebasket—although she knew the missing page wasn't likely to be there. Nowhere did she find it. What she sought simply wasn't in the apartment. And it wasn't at Arrow, either.

Leslie collapsed on the sofa and tried to decide what she should do. It would be no problem to print out the missing page, now that she knew what hoops she must jump through to do so. But if the page could have been taken by someone intent on selling the information to a competing company, she had a duty to report its loss.

I suppose I have to tell Andrew Miller, she acknowledged—she really had no other choice. But before she did, Leslie resolved to confront Hampton directly about the matter. If she could see his eyes when she asked him about it, she'd know if he'd taken the page or not.

Past that point, Leslie refused to think.

&

"I didn't know that cooking was one of your talents, Miss Redmond," Hampton Travis said that evening as Barbara Redmond set plates of lasagna and salad before him.

"I always heard that the way to a man's heart was through his stomach," Barbara replied with light sarcasm.

"No, really, what's the inspiration for this sudden burst of culinary activity? I thought you were strictly a dine-out or take-out cook."

Barbara's tone was all business. "We shouldn't be seen together again."

"Oh? What's happened?"

"I saw Leslie Christopher today about a security violation and she asked if I knew you. She must have seen us together at the restaurant or the other night at the ice cream parlor."

"What security violation?"

Barbara told Hampton about the printout, and he nodded. "I saw it last night. She brought it home with her."

"And?" Barbara prompted, nettled that Hampton never seemed willing to share all he knew with her, even though they were supposed to be working together.

"And probably showed it to somebody."

"Just somebody? You don't know who?" Barbara sounded incredulous.

"No. I'd just gotten to her apartment last night when someone she didn't want me to see rang the doorbell and she pushed me out the back door. I tried to trail him when he came out, but the Willows' security guard had other ideas."

"How awful!" Barbara said, although her smile showed a certain amount of amusement at Hampton's discomfort. "You didn't get anything on him at all?"

"I could tell he was a large man, but it was too dark to see his face. I'd think it might have been her boss, if he weren't in the hospital—he was about the same height as

Richard Meredith."

"What are we going to do now?"

"Wait and see what Les—Miss Christopher does. The material she had there last night wouldn't be important enough for anyone to risk passing on. When she can come up with something that is, they'll make their move."

"What do you want me to do?"

"Watch the printout requests and call me immediately when she does another run. And let me know who she's hired for the head scientist slot."

"It'd be a lot simpler if it could have been you. I still don't see why you pulled back from it."

"You know how often I've been called away lately—those absences would be hard to justify."

"Maybe, but I think you had other reasons as well. What about the man who was at her apartment last night?"

"I have a hunch he's either our man or that he'll lead us to the one who is. I think it's time to let the Feds in on what's going on."

❧

While Leslie ate her solitary supper, she considered what she'd say to Hampton when she called him. She didn't dare ask him to come to her apartment; it'd be better to meet him in public, in broad daylight, so he couldn't construe it as an invitation for him to kiss her again. As much as she had enjoyed it, Leslie knew there was no place in her life for that kind of relationship now—especially with a man who could be more interested in VIRCO's secrets than in her.

Leslie called the number she had always used for Hampton and, as usual, got his answering service. Hanging up without leaving a message, she found the "private" number he'd given her in the pocket of the jeans she'd worn the night before. Leslie let the phone ring many times, but there was no answer.

Typical, Leslie thought as she replaced the receiver. Hampton had said he wanted to help her, then he disappeared. *Well, I can always try later,* she thought—but it was a good thing she wasn't depending on him for immediate help.

❧

It was nearly ten o'clock by the time Hampton returned to his apartment. He hadn't intended to stay at Barbara's so long, but they had seemed to have an unusual number of things to discuss, and the time had passed very quickly. The food had been surprisingly good too—a pleasant change for Hampton, accustomed to quick bachelor meals eaten out or made in the apartment with the aid of his major staples—a microwave oven and can opener.

A man could grow to like that, he thought, but it wasn't Barbara Redmond he envisioned in his kitchen. Could Leslie cook? Hampton didn't know—nor did he care. Staying away from her for the next few days wouldn't be easy—

The telephone rang, and Hampton sighed, took a deep breath, and answered it in his usual way. "Travis speaking."

"Hampton, this is Leslie. I know it's late, but I called earlier and got no answer."

"Leslie! I just got in. Are you all right?"

"Yes, but I need to talk to you. Can you meet me in the Arrow cafeteria tomorrow around eleven?"

"I suppose so," he said, quickly thinking of ways to rearrange his schedule. "What's this about?"

There was a pause, then she said, "I can't tell you now."

"All right. I'll be there."

Leslie thanked him and hung up, leaving Hampton to wonder what she wanted. Whatever it was, he was glad he'd see her again so soon.

≈

In the lull between the coffee break and lunch hour, the Arrow cafeteria was usually deserted. When Leslie arrived the next morning, Hampton was already seated at a small table near the rear, the only occupant of the vast room.

"Am I late?" she asked as he stood and pulled out her chair.

"No. I was so eager to see you I got here early. Can I get you coffee?"

"Yes, please." While Hampton was gone Leslie moved her chair slightly so she'd be seated exactly opposite him. She wanted to see the look in his eyes when she confronted him.

"Here you are," he said, setting an old-fashioned white china mug before her. "But be careful—Arrow's brew packs quite a jolt."

"In Los Angeles they claimed that the first rocket fuel was the scientists' coffee," Leslie said, smiling at the memory.

"Do you ever wish you were still in Los Angeles?"

"No. I've been so busy here I really haven't had any time for regrets."

"I'm glad you feel that way. You certainly seem to be doing a good job."

Leslie looked down at her coffee in an effort to stifle the emotions that the look in Hampton's eyes were stirring in her. "That's part of why I wanted to see you today. I need to ask you something related to my job."

"Fire away," Hampton said pleasantly.

Leslie raised her head and stared into his blue eyes. "A page is missing from my VIRCO printout. Did you take it?"

For a moment Hampton resembled a statue frozen in time, his coffee cup suspended near his mouth, his eyes staring back into hers with shocked surprise. Then he looked away as he set his cup down on the table without drinking from it. "What makes you ask?"

"You were there. You handled it."

"Therefore I must be guilty."

"You haven't answered me," Leslie said, her cheeks warming. "A simple yes or no will do."

"I don't suppose pleading the Fifth Amendment would help, would it?"

"Not if you've already incriminated yourself."

"Have I done that?" Hampton's eyes locked on hers, his message clear. "No, Miss Christopher, I didn't take anything from your printout."

Leslie looked at him closely and sighed, wondering how much her wanting to believe him inclined her to accept his denial. "Are you positive? Maybe a page fell into your coat pocket when you helped me pick them up?"

Hampton patted his pockets. "Nope, there's nothing here but an old parking ticket," he said, opening his pockets for her inspection.

"All right, I believe you. But I don't see how it could just disappear into thin air."

"Was that page so important? Surely you must have some kind of backup."

"It's not that," Leslie began, then stopped. If she said

more, she would be getting into sensitive areas she couldn't discuss.

"I don't have it, but I have a good idea who might."

Leslie looked at Hampton closely. "Who?"

"I wasn't your only visitor last night. You might ask that other person about your missing page."

Leslie glanced at her wristwatch and stood. "I must get back to the office. I'm sorry if I was rude."

Hampton chuckled. "I'm not sure that 'rude' covers being accused of larceny. But I hope you find whatever it is that you lost."

"So do I."

At the cafeteria entrance, Leslie offered her hand. "Thanks for coming here," she said formally.

"The pleasure was mine, Miss Christopher," Hampton said. He took her hand in both of his instead of shaking it. "If you need me, you know how to reach me."

Leslie watched Hampton turn in his visitor's badge, and with a last wave in her direction, he left the building. She was almost positive that he hadn't taken the page, but it hadn't reappeared, nor was it likely to. Leslie supposed she had no choice but to report the loss to the FBI.

The number that Agent Miller had given her and warned her not to write down rang so many times that Leslie almost hung up when she heard the click of the connection. "Hello."

"This is Leslie Christopher. I think there might be a problem."

"I'll see you tonight at six," he said and hung up.

❧

Andrew Miller was punctual as usual, and as usual he appeared to search the apartment before he spoke.

"What's this all about, Miss Christopher?"

"A page of my VIRCO printout is missing."

Miller frowned his displeasure. "Missing! How could you be so careless?"

"I wasn't careless," Leslie said, unexpectedly put on the defensive. "I had it the night you were here, and the next morning it was gone. I've looked here and at the office, and it's definitely not in either place."

"Who else saw it?"

"Some of my office staff—but that was after I took it back."

"There was no one else?" he asked, and Leslie lowered her eyes under his searching gaze.

"There was one other person—a man saw the printout from across the room, but I don't think he took anything."

"Ah." Miller brought out the now-familiar notebook. He wet his lips as he asked for her visitor's name.

"Hampton Travis," she forced herself to say.

"Travis!" he exclaimed, frowning. "I should have known."

"What will you do now?" Leslie asked, not liking Miller's expression.

"For now, nothing. He won't be able to make much of the budget figures yet. But in a little while, after more comes in, we'll make our move. And this time, we'll catch him."

"Surely you can't think that Hampton Travis is the Arrow leak—he hasn't even worked there in ages."

Miller frowned and shook his head. "Let us worry about that, young lady."

"I want nothing to do with any entrapment," Leslie said firmly.

"I'm afraid you have no choice—you can't quit now. I'm sure you wouldn't want to wind up with a reprimand on your record for violating security, would you?"

"No, but I don't like this. I'm not suited for intrigue."

Miller chuckled as if she'd told him an especially good joke. "You have no idea just how ideally suited you are for this job. I'll be in touch."

Leslie closed the door behind him and leaned against it, a feeling of dread knotting her stomach. What damage had she already done to Hampton—and what more did Miller expect her to do?

Then with almost physical force, Leslie recalled that the agent's comment about the budget figures. *I didn't tell him what page was missing,* she realized. *Did he know, or was it just a lucky guess?*

Leslie sat down hard in the nearest chair and put her head in her hands. Something was not right about this whole business, but she couldn't put her finger on exactly what. *I need Mr. Meredith's advice,* she thought, and wished that his surgery could have been postponed until after the VIRCO proposal had been safely submitted.

Leslie glanced at her watch and noted that she still had time to get to the hospital before the end of visiting hours. *It won't hurt anything for me to go see him,* she told herself as she slung her purse over her shoulder and started out the door. At the least, she had good news to report about VIRCO staffing. At the most, if her boss seemed up to it, she would tell him about Andrew Miller.

Leslie found Richard Meredith sitting up in bed in his flower-filled room, watching a television documentary about a recent Space Shuttle launch. His daughter immediately rose to offer Leslie her chair.

"I was just about to leave, anyway," Alicia said.

"How is the patient?" Leslie asked.

His pallor and pinched look indicated that he was still in considerable pain, but Mr. Meredith made an effort to smile. "'Patient' is a good word for it, I suppose. I'm ready to start feeling better any minute now, starting yesterday."

"The doctor says he really needed the surgery, Miss Christopher," his daughter said. "Dad just doesn't know how to be sick."

"Does anyone ever know how?" he asked wryly.

"When do you have to go back to school?" Leslie asked, aware that Alicia Meredith must already have missed quite a few of her college classes.

"In a few days," Alicia replied. "My profs have been quite understanding, but I don't dare push their generosity much further." She turned to her father and smiled, touching his hand. "I really do need to say goodnight, Dad. I'll be back tomorrow."

"It's nice to see you again," Leslie said. "Good luck on making up your work."

"I don't believe in luck," Mr. Meredith said as his daughter left the room.

"Or rather, I suppose I should say I believe that we make our own luck by working hard."

"Quite true," Leslie agreed, "and everyone in Special Projects has been doing just that on VIRCO." Briefly, Leslie sketched the progress she'd made in staffing, and Mr. Meredith nodded, looking pleased.

"I'm sorry I haven't been able to help, but it sounds as if you have everything under control," he said.

"Well, almost everything." Leslie paused, unsure how to broach what might be a very painful subject.

"Now, what?" he asked, and Leslie searched for the best way to tell him what had happened.

"I think the FBI is about to ask me to help catch a possible security leak in the company," she said. "I'm not looking forward to it."

Mr. Meredith closed his eyes for a moment, and Leslie feared that she had upset him. But when he opened them, his whole appearance seemed more alert. "Don't worry about it. These people know what they're doing, and we've needed to catch whoever has been betraying Arrow's confidences. I'm just sorry I can't be there to help."

"Then I should do whatever they ask me to do, even if I don't understand why?"

A half smile crossed his face, then Richard Meredith sighed. "'Ours is not to reason why,'" he quoted. "Who knows, you might even get a promotion if this works out."

I don't want any promotion, Leslie thought, *I just want to be out of the counter-espionage business and for Hampton Travis to be cleared.*

"I can see you're tired," she said aloud. "I won't bother you any further with business."

"It's no bother," Mr. Meredith said. "By the way, Alicia told me that you were here during my surgery. I really appreciate that."

"If we'd known when it was going to be, more of us would have come. When I left Arrow, Sally wanted me to tell you she was praying for you."

Mr. Meredith nodded. "A lot of people were. Thank Sally and tell her I still need all the prayers I can get. I'm afraid I'm not out of the woods yet."

On her way out, Leslie stopped at the nurses' station and asked when Mr. Meredith would be discharged.

"That depends on how well he does," was the noncommittal answer.

"A few days, a few weeks, what is usual?" Leslie persisted.

"Probably no less than a week, providing all goes well. Mr. Meredith's doctor will make that decision."

Put in her place by the nurse's tone, Leslie thanked her and left, feeling no better about her relationship with the FBI than she had before.

❧

Leslie glanced at the time line she had taped to her office wall, knowing all too well that her time was running out. It would take many workers' expertise and energy—and Leslie's wise management—to put the pieces together by the NASA deadline. She only hoped that she could work without any more distractions—from Andrew Miller or Hampton Travis or anyone else—and accomplish what everyone expected of her.

At the weekly staff meeting Leslie looked around the room and wondered how many of the VIRCO team doubted her ability to manage Arrow's bid, particularly in the absence of the Special Projects chief. But if they had any doubts, they kept them unvoiced. The newest members of the team seemed to be working well with the others. Without telling them that someone in the Arrow organization might possibly be selling information to others, she stressed the need for continuing tight security.

"I learned the hard way that we can't even print out documents without the security system finding out," she said, using her own case to let them know how seriously security breaches, even innocent ones, were taken.

Everyone seemed to accept the need for the tightened

security, and Leslie was satisfied that her VIRCO team was completely loyal. If someone was selling information—and Leslie still wasn't convinced that was the case—it certainly wasn't anyone on her staff.

Leslie concluded the meeting punctually on the hour, and as the others filed out, she felt as tired as if she had been doing hard physical labor all morning.

"How about a cup of coffee?" Sally asked. "You look beat."

"I feel that way, too, but I need more than coffee at this point. I think I'll just sit here awhile and try to collect my wits."

"All right. Shall I hold your calls?"

"Yes, unless it's an emergency."

After Sally left, Leslie kicked off her high heels, leaned back in her swivel chair, propped her feet on the table, and closed her eyes. She had rested that way only a short while when Sally came back into the conference room.

"I'm sorry, but you have a caller that won't take no for an answer."

"Who is it?" Leslie's eyes flew open, and her heart began to beat faster as she imagined that Andrew Miller was about to ask her to do something more for the FBI.

"I don't know, but he insisted that you'd want to talk to him. Shall I transfer the call here?"

"No. I have to go back to my office sooner or later," Leslie said. "I'll take it there."

A short time later Leslie picked up her desk phone, steeling herself for Andrew Miller's voice. "Leslie Christopher," she said crisply.

"Sorry to bother you at work, but I wondered if you'd found that lost item."

Surprised that Hampton Travis would call her at Arrow, Leslie tried not to show it. "Why do you ask?"

"I knew you were worried about it. I thought perhaps you'd taken my advice."

"What about?" Leslie asked.

"Asking the other party about the missing item."

"It's really none of your business, Dr. Travis," Leslie said. On the other end of the line, Hampton chuckled, but his tone was serious when he spoke again.

"So you say." He paused for a moment. "I'm going to be tied up here for a while longer, and there's a telephone number I want to give you."

"What kind of number?" Leslie asked. In the background she could hear the hum of machinery, and she realized Hampton must be calling her from wherever he was working.

"It's a private emergency line to the local FBI office. Do you have something to write with?"

Leslie nodded and reached for a pen, then realized that Hampton couldn't see the gesture. "Yes. But I don't understand—"

"Never mind," he said brusquely. "This is a toll-free call, so it's got a lot of digits." He read out the number, then made her repeat it. As she did so, Leslie heard someone calling Hampton's name.

"I've got to run," he said. "I'll contact you the minute I get back. Try to stay out of trouble until then, will you?"

Without waiting for her to reply, he hung up. Leslie imagined him working on someone else's problems and sighed. *I wish Hampton had stayed here,* she thought. The number he had given her was familiar, Leslie thought as she tucked it into her skirt pocket. Then she remembered—it was the same number Mr. Meredith had given her.

Every man I meet seems obsessed with giving me a telephone number, she thought. And it was certainly ironic that both Mr. Meredith and Hampton had given her the same telephone number for the FBI, when she was already working with one of their agents.

After sitting for a moment thinking about the look in Hampton's blue eyes the last time she had seen him, Leslie buzzed Sally.

"I ought to report you," she said accusingly.

"Whatever for?" Sally asked with offended innocence.

"I asked you to hold my calls."

"He said he was a personal friend, and I thought maybe he'd ask you out. You've been pretty down all week, you know."

"He can't—he's been working out of town."

"Oh," Sally said, obviously disappointed. "He has a great phone voice, though. Since he's not available, how about coming to my house tomorrow night for a pot-luck supper?"

Leslie almost said no automatically, but something told her not to this time. *I need to keep busy,* she thought. And if she wasn't at home, Andrew Miller couldn't contact her.

"All right, but what's pot-luck, and when do you want me there?" she asked.

Sally laughed. "They don't have dinners in California where everyone brings something to share? Sometimes it's called 'covered-dish'—but you don't have to bring anything—just be at my house about six-thirty."

It sounds awful, Leslie thought, but after she had agreed to go, she found that she was almost looking forward to it.

nine

Told to dress casually, Leslie chose black stirrup slacks, worn with flats and a long blue cotton sweater top. Despite Sally's admonition not to bring anything, she had stopped at bakery for whole wheat rolls. It was fully dark by the time Leslie finally found Sally's address in the maze of a subdivision. To her surprise, more than a dozen cars were already there, and Leslie had to park three houses down.

I probably shouldn't be doing this, she thought as she rang the doorbell. But when Sally appeared, wearing an old-fashioned, bib-topped apron, her welcome smile made Leslie feel more at ease.

"Oh, thank you for bringing the rolls—one of gals that was bringing bread couldn't come at the last minute, so this is just what we needed. Dale, Harriet—come here and meet Leslie Christopher, from Arrow."

"Dale" turned out to be a distinguished-looking older man with salt-and-pepper hair. Leslie recognized him as Dr. Dale Davis, a lab director at Marshall Space Flight Center, the NASA facility in Huntsville. "Harriet" was about Leslie's age with the kind of face that seemed plain until she smiled, lighting up the entire room.

"I've heard a lot about you, Leslie," Harriet said. "We've been trying to get Sally to bring you to our class."

"Class?" Leslie repeated.

"The singles Bible study group at Glenview," Dale said.

"Of course, you'd have to listen to me, but that part doesn't last too long."

"Don't let him fool you—he's the best Bible teacher I ever met."

Bible teacher—Glenview. Now understanding what Sally had gotten her into, Leslie looked around, prepared to glare at her, but she'd disappeared.

"Come on and meet the others," Harriet said, taking Leslie's hand. In short order she met two teachers, three engineers, a real estate agent, a couple of women who identified themselves as homemakers, a reference librarian, and a doctor.

"Someone who can really fix what ails you, not a scientist," Dale added as he made the final introduction.

Despite her initial misgivings, Leslie soon felt almost as if she had known these people forever. And when they joined hands as Dale said a prayer of thanks for the food, Leslie felt a strange warmth that she'd seldom known before.

"Aren't you glad you came tonight?" Sally asked when, after helping clean up in the kitchen, Leslie prepared to leave.

"Yes," Leslie admitted. "Although you did sort of get me here on false pretenses."

"I didn't mean to," Sally said. "I just thought if you knew some of our group you'd feel more comfortable about coming to Glenview on Sunday morning."

"Oh, I'm going to do that too, am I?" Leslie asked.

"I hope so." Sally put a hand lightly on Leslie's arm. "You've done very well in your job, but I know something's been troubling you lately. Maybe you can't tell me about it, but whatever it is, God is always there to anchor you. I think you'll feel that at Glenview."

"We all have our bad days," Leslie murmured. More than once she had wished she could confide in Sally, but she had never seriously considered doing so. Even if she hadn't promised to keep silent, it wouldn't be fair to burden anyone else with her worries.

Sally laughed ruefully and shook her head. "Bad days! I had bad weeks and bad months, until I realized that all my crying and blaming God for Jeff's death wouldn't bring him back. The people at Glenview almost literally dragged me to the singles class—but connecting with it is the best thing that's happened to me since I lost Jeff."

"They do seem to be a caring group," Leslie said.

Sally nodded. "Yes, and you'll meet even more of the class Sunday morning. The ones here tonight are in my interest group—there are many others. Some are younger and some older, widowed, divorced, or never married— we've got them all."

"I'm not looking for a husband," Leslie reminded Sally.

"Neither are most of the Glenview singles, including me," Sally said. "Of course, there've been several weddings, but that's not what it's about."

"I'm not looking for a church, either."

"No obligation," Sally assured her. "We meet at nine-thirty every Sunday."

"Glenview's that big round church over in the valley, isn't it?"

Sally nodded. "The same. Be ready at 9:15—I'll come by for you."

"That sounds like an order," Leslie said.

Sally smiled. "At Arrow, you're always my boss. On weekends—"

"I still do what I like," Leslie said. "Thanks, Sally. I'll see you Sunday, then."

Leslie worked all day on Saturday, cleaning her apartment and doing her laundry. She hoped that Hampton would call and feared that Andrew Miller might instead, but the telephone never rang all day long. After she had washed her hair and gotten ready for bed, Leslie wished she hadn't been so quick to say that she'd go to Sally's church. It had been years since she'd attended a regular church service, and the few memories she had of them were not pleasant.

But Leslie had agreed to go, and she wouldn't go back on her word.

❧

Whatever Leslie might have thought about Glenview, its reality far surpassed her imagination. The church was huge, yet everyone seemed to know everyone else, or greeted them as if they did, anyway. The singles class members wore ID badges—"Just like at work," Sally joked as she pinned Leslie's to her suit lapel. And while she recognized a few faces from Friday night, most there were new to her.

After a brief fellowship time with coffee, Dale came forward to lead the group in prayer, after which he opened his Bible and began to read Psalm 121. Leslie hadn't thought to bring her own Bible—which she'd moved from California and put away in her bookcase—so she looked on with Sally.

"'I will lift up mine eyes unto the hills, from whence cometh my help. My help cometh from the Lord, which made heaven and earth. He will not suffer thy foot to be moved; he that keepeth Israel shall neither slumber nor sleep. The Lord is thy keeper: the Lord is thy shade upon thy right hand. The sun shall not smite thee by day, nor the moon by night.

"The Lord shall preserve thee from all evil: he shall preserve thy soul. The Lord shall preserve thy going out and thy coming in from this time forth, and even for evermore.'"

Leslie recalled Hampton's comment that people had always thought that God lived on mountaintops. Certainly the beauty of the mountains that formed the backdrop for the city was proof of the magnificence of God's creation.

Keeping the book open on his knees, Dale began talking about the historical background of the Psalm and the trust the verses expressed. He told them about some times in his life when he had had to learn to rely on God's protection and asked those in the group who had similar experiences to share theirs as well. Soon, nearly everyone had joined in a lively discussion of the Psalm's application to modern life.

Intellectually, Leslie understood what they were saying, but in her heart she had doubts. How could the Lord preserve anyone from evil when they still had to live in an evil world? *Things must have been different in those long-ago times,* Leslie concluded.

The Bible study hour ended, and Sally ushered Leslie into the huge circular sanctuary. "I always sit here—force of habit, I suppose," Sally said when they were settled in a pew near the front of the church.

"It's so big," Leslie said, watching as a robed choir filed into a loft behind the raised pulpit platform.

"Wait until you hear the acoustics—they're first-rate."

Then the minister entered, and with a shock Leslie realized it was the man who'd prayed for Mr. Meredith in the hospital. "I didn't know Mr. Meredith was a member of this church," she whispered to Sally, who merely nodded in reply.

The music—provided by choir, piano, organ, and a small orchestra—soared to the round dome of the sanctuary, and when a young couple sang a duet to a taped accompaniment, Leslie felt chills march up and down her spine. For the sermon, coincidentally or not, the pastor also chose a text from Psalms. As he read it, Leslie was reminded of the time she'd heard Hampton quote some of the same words.

"'O Lord, our Lord, how excellent is thy name in all the earth! who has set thy glory above the heavens. Out of the mouths of babes and sucklings thou hast ordained strength because of thine enemies, that thou mightest still the enemy and the avenger. When I consider thy heavens, the work of thy fingers, the moon and the stars, which thou hast ordained; What is man that thou art mindful of him? and the son of man, that thou visitest him?'"

A tide of emotion washed over Leslie, and fervently she wished that Hampton could be there with her to hear the very words he had once quoted to her. In this place, it almost seemed that she could sense the presence of God near her.

Help me, God, she began. Past that, Leslie hardly knew what to say. She tried to follow the pastor's words, but often found her mind wandering, anticipating with dread what lay in store for her in the days ahead.

Perhaps there's some measure of comfort to be found in a church, but these people have nothing to do with me, she told herself, and deliberately Leslie resolved not to give in to the strange new emotion she felt while the choir sang softly during the altar call.

Outside in the bright, cold November sunshine, Leslie blinked as if she were awakening from a dream and assured Sally she had enjoyed the services.

"Next Sunday you can come on your own, now that you know where it is," Sally said when she let her out at the Willows.

"Yes," Leslie agreed, although she had already decided not to make a habit of churchgoing—at least not until the VIRCO business was straightened out.

Then maybe I can have a real life, she told herself.

৵

A large portion of the VIRCO proposal came together in the next week as Leslie worked nonstop coordinating, delegating, and checking all the details.

Leslie had menacing dreams about the FBI agent. And as the days passed, she wished he would go ahead and assign her final task and have done with it. She found herself startling nervously when the telephone rang, expecting each time that Andrew Miller was calling to say it was time to set the trap.

The most critical period would be the week before the proposals were sent to NASA, when there was still time to alter them before the pages and pages of documents were finally printed and bound in the manner prescribed by the Request for Proposal. At last the end was in sight— except for a few of the more complicated engineering studies and graphics, the proposal was basically finished— and still she hadn't been contacted by Andrew Miller. But just after lunch the next Friday Sally buzzed her on the intercom.

"An FBI agent is on his way to your office. Quick, hide the evidence!"

"I hope he can't hear you," Leslie said, aware that Sally would never say such a thing if the agent hadn't been well out of earshot.

Leslie was surprised that Andrew Miller would come to her office, since he had made such a point to stay away from it before. But she had an even bigger surprise when she opened her office door.

"Miss Christopher? I'm Jack Taylor," he said, displaying his badge. "We met when I ran your security check."

"Yes, I remember. Please have a seat." Leslie sat behind her desk and waited for him to state his business.

"I've been asked to check out a possible security leak here at Arrow, and I think you can help."

"Security leak?" Leslie hoped she didn't sound as dazed as she felt.

"Yes. Mr. Meredith may have mentioned it—I discussed it with him earlier and neither of us thought there was enough evidence to take more drastic measures—until now."

Mr. Taylor stopped talking and regarded Leslie as if he expected some response to what he had told her.

"What sort of security leak?"

"We're not sure, and that's where you come in. We know that you printed out a preliminary report on the VIRCO proposal and took it to your apartment. We believe that someone asked you to do it, and that a part of the material you brought home turned up missing. Is that correct?"

He doesn't need to ask, Leslie thought, certain that her face betrayed her consternation. She nodded.

"Would you like to tell me about it?" he asked, sounding like a counselor trying to soothe a troubled patient.

"I didn't want to do it—I always felt something wasn't right about it. But the FBI asked me, and the agent made it clear I was expected to help."

"The FBI? I can assure you that you weren't dealing with any of our agents."

Leslie felt as if she had been physically struck. *How could I have been so stupid?* She forced herself to speak. "He had a badge just like yours. I had no way of knowing—"

"What name did he use?"

"Andrew Miller. I suppose that's probably as phony as his badge."

"What does he look like?" he asked, making notes as she spoke.

"He's a short and stocky man with a ruddy complexion—maybe five-eight, around two hundred pounds, I'd say—middle-aged. His hair is light brown, and thinning on top."

"That's an unusually good description. Do you know where he lives?"

"No, but he gave me a phone number where I could call him. I used it once."

"Do you remember it?" he asked, and Leslie repeated it.

"Excellent! When did you last see this man?"

"The night after I brought home the printout. When I couldn't find the other page I called Mr. Miller to tell him it was missing, and he came over."

"Has he contacted you since then?"

"No, but he said he'd be in touch before our proposal went out. He said I'd have to do one last thing so the FBI could catch whoever was leaking the information."

"Do you know what he'll ask you to do?"

Leslie shook her head. "I assume it would have to do with printing out some of the key parts of our proposal. He said something about using it as bait."

"Bait, indeed!" Jack Taylor slapped the notebook against his hand as he closed it.

"Will you arrest him now?"

Jack Taylor shook his head. "No. All he could be charged with now is impersonating a Federal agent, and that's not enough. We want to catch him accepting Arrow documents."

"How will you do that?"

"With your help, I hope, Miss Christopher."

"That's what Mr. Miller said, and I was stupid enough to be taken in by it. Why should I make the same mistake twice?"

"You thought you were doing the right thing then— that doesn't matter. Now you have the chance to help your company and put away a criminal at the same time."

"What do I have to do?" Leslie asked, feeling suddenly chilled.

"When he contacts you, go along with whatever he suggests. All you have to do is meet with him. We'll take care of the rest."

"It seems that I've heard that before too. What if something goes wrong and he passes our material to someone else before you can arrest him? We could very well lose the right to compete for this contract."

"Make up some of the material—real enough so that he won't be suspicious, yet fake enough so that Arrow's real proposal wouldn't be affected if it should fall into the wrong hands—which of course won't happen, anyway. Will you do this for us?"

Leslie was silent for a moment, then she sighed and shrugged. "Yes, but I must tell you that I don't look forward to it at all."

For the first time, the agent smiled. "I'd be worried about your sanity if you did. Here, take this," he added as he stood. He handed her a standard business card bearing two phone numbers. "If I'm out of the office, the second one is my beeper number."

"I just hope he contacts me soon. I want this business to be finished."

"Of course you do," he said sympathetically. "And one other thing," Jack Taylor added from the doorway. "No one else is to know about this."

In spite of herself, Leslie laughed. "You FBI agents are all alike," she said, surprised that she could salvage any glimmer of humor from the situation. "That's exactly what Andrew Miller—or whoever he is—told me."

"I'm glad you can still smile. It won't be much longer now—try not to worry. And call me the moment you hear from him, day or night."

"I will," Leslie promised.

As she closed the door after Jack Taylor, Leslie leaned against it for a moment, her anger growing stronger as she thought of the way she had let the man who called himself Andrew Miller take her in.

Then another thought came to her mind. How had Jack Taylor found out about it? Only one person could have pieced together what had happened—*Hampton Travis.*

She should have asked Jack Taylor about him, she thought as she sat back down at her desk. Hampton must be involved in some way, but how?

Leslie found it hard to focus her attention on the figures she was supposed to be reviewing. They swam before her eyes, then cleared as another name came to her mind. *Barbara Redmond!* She'd seen the Arrow security worker with Hampton several times, and Barbara knew that Leslie had made the printout. Hampton no doubt had told Barbara he'd seen it, and she must have passed the information on to Jack Taylor.

Where Hampton fit into the whole business Leslie didn't know, but she dismissed any idea that he might be the security leak that Arrow had asked the FBI to find.

Who was Andrew Miller, really? Leslie thought that Jack Taylor should have no trouble identifying him from the information she had furnished—and she dearly hoped that he would get what he deserved.

If I knew how to, I'd pray that this whole business would end soon, Leslie thought.

❧

Later that day, Leslie had just finished proofreading the first portion of the proposal when she finally received the call she had both hoped for and dreaded.

"Will you be at home about nine this evening?" the man who called himself Andrew Miller asked.

"Yes," Leslie replied, trying very hard to sound normal.

He hung up without saying anything further, and Leslie immediately called Jack Taylor's office number.

"This is Leslie Christopher. Andrew Miller is coming to my apartment at nine o'clock tonight."

"Did he ask you to bring anything home?"

"No. He'll probably tell me what he wants tonight. Have

you found out who he really is?"

"Not yet, but we're working on it."

"I hope I can pull this off without telling that slug what I think of him."

"I'm sure you can. The less you say to him, the better. We'll be in the vicinity, watching. When he leaves, I'll knock four times on your apartment door. And by the way, don't use your home phone to call us—it might be bugged."

"Surely you're not serious!"

"We haven't had a chance to check it out yet, but as slick as this operator is, it's a distinct possibility."

"Just like in the spy novels," Leslie said without enthusiasm.

Jack Taylor chuckled. "Almost. Remember that this will soon be over."

After he had hung up, Leslie remembered that she hadn't asked him about Hampton. It was just as well, she thought, There was no point in dragging his name into the situation—it might cause needless trouble.

Leslie ate an early supper and tried to watch television while waiting for the man she knew as Andrew Miller to arrive, but she couldn't concentrate and soon switched off the set. She had just started to work a crossword puzzle when the doorbell rang, just before 7:30.

"You're early," Leslie said when she opened the door.

Ignoring her remark, Andrew Miller once more looked carefully around the apartment. "Your proposal should be ready to go by now."

"All except the final proofing. It's been a real struggle to finish on time."

"Yes, I'm sure it has, and the last thing you need now is

for someone to give all that hard-earned information to a competitor, right?"

"Do you still think someone will?" Leslie forced herself to say.

"That's why I'm here. We believe that with your help we can now catch the guilty party."

"What do you want me to do?"

"Are you familiar with invisible dye?"

"No. Is it like invisible ink?"

"It's used to mark money—invisible until it rubs off on the hands of anyone who touches it, then it turns a dark purple that doesn't wash off."

"I don't understand."

"You don't have to," he said impatiently. "Just bring the engineering abstract and the cost figures. I'll treat them, then you take them back to Arrow and leave the proposal in plain sight in the staff room. That purple dye will lead directly to the security leak—and we'll have the proof to put him—or her—away."

He must think that I'm really stupid to fall for such a crazy scheme, Leslie thought. Then she remembered how she'd been so easily duped into thinking Miller was an FBI agent and realized he would naturally think she would continue to go along with anything he said.

"Do you think it'll work?" Leslie said aloud.

"It'll do the job," he replied, looking self-satisfied. "I wouldn't be surprised if you wind up with a promotion as a result of your cooperation."

"I just want this to be over," Leslie said honestly.

"Quite so. Now here is what you must do—"

Again it was what she *must* do.

"You're quite specific about the information I should

bring you," she said. "Are you certain that you need that much?"

"There has to be enough information to make the risk worthwhile," he said, again looking pained at having to explain it to her. "It shouldn't take you long to get those pages together."

"I'll have to unbind a copy. Documentation will wonder why one is missing."

"Not if you photocopy the pages first," he said, again speaking as if she were an extremely slow learner and he the patient teacher. "Do you understand what you are to do?"

Leslie nodded.

"Good," he said, all but patting her on the head as a stupid little girl who'd finally recited her lesson correctly. "I'll see you tomorrow evening, then."

Andrew Miller hadn't been gone more than five minutes when four knocks sounded on her door in rapid succession. Leslie looked through the peephole to make sure it was Jack Taylor before she let him in.

"He was early," he greeted her. "How did it go?"

"From your standpoint, very well, I suppose. I've agreed to bring home several summary documents—the heart of the proposal—tomorrow night."

"Great! I presume you'll be able to doctor the material."

"Yes, but I'll have to be careful that no one sees me changing those figures we've been so careful with—they'd think I'd lost my mind."

"At least you have one to lose," Jack Taylor said with a rare smile. "In my business, we sometimes struggle to hang on to ours."

"I can imagine," Leslie said, wondering how anyone could survive on a steady diet of tension and intrigue. But to them, her career and problems that came with it was obviously not ordinary.

"We'll assume that he'll come back here tomorrow night. I'll need a key to your apartment. Unless he changes the plan—call me immediately if he does—we'll be hiding in the apartment when you get home. As soon as he takes the papers, we'll grab him. Then you can go back to being a full-time private citizen."

"That can't happen soon enough to suit me," Leslie said.

She had never spoken more sincerely in her life.

ten

As soon as she got to work the next day, Leslie disassembled one of the preliminary proposals and selected a few of the key pages. She didn't have to worry about changing all of them, since Andrew Miller—or whoever he was—wouldn't have time to look at them before he was arrested. But the top few pages ought to look good, and with these she took special pains.

Leslie finished her task well before noon, replaced the original sheets, and sent the proposal back to word processing, which was still working on last-minute changes. The copied sheets she put into her briefcase, then locked and stowed it in her file cabinet, which she also locked. Satisfied that the pages were secure, Leslie turned her attention to last-minute proposal details.

"We're not in sync on some of the figures," Pat Wentworth told her at lunch. "I don't know how it happened, but a few of the engineering calculations just don't match up."

"Recheck them," Leslie suggested. "Let's hope it's just some kind of small error in arithmetic."

"There are no small errors in space," said Bob McLaren as he joined them. "It's a very unforgiving environment."

"I'd like you to take a look at the figures," Pat told Bob. "I don't know how they got so haywire, but we can't submit the proposal if the math doesn't work."

"We're running out of time, gentlemen," Leslie reminded them. Such a glitch at this stage would've usually upset her, but compared to what she faced that night, this problem seemed almost minor.

"We know. I tried to get Hampton Travis for a consult, but I haven't been able to locate him."

At the mention of Hampton's name, Leslie's head came up and she looked questioningly at Pat. "He's out of town," she said.

Bob McLaren nodded. "Yeah, we know—we tried to call the outfit he went out to work for and the stupid robot that answers their phone said Dr. Travis was unavailable. When I tried to leave a message for him, it bleeped at me and hung up. I don't think that electronic pile of junk works."

"Yeah," Pat agreed, "just like everyone says—'How come we can send a man to the moon, but we can't make a decent answering machine?'"

Leslie laughed with them, but the mention of Hampton's name reminded her that she missed him very much.

A last-minute flap in another project on which Leslie was filling in for Mr. Meredith kept her from her own desk until after five o'clock. Since no messages awaited her, Leslie presumed that the plans for the evening hadn't changed. By the time Leslie left the building, most of the other employees were gone. Walking to the parking lot, her head down against a biting wind, Leslie recalled a bit of a poem she had once read that described "No sun, No warmth, November." On these cold days, Leslie really missed the Southern California weather. Yet, despite all that had happened to her in Huntsville, she had no desire to return there.

Leslie put her briefcase in the trunk, unlocked her car,

and slid behind the wheel, and then she closed the door. She had just fitted her key into the ignition when, suddenly aware that someone was standing beside the car, she turned her head and saw Andrew Miller.

More surprised than frightened, Leslie rolled down her window. "Is something wrong?"

"No. Did you get the material?"

Leslie's mind raced as she tried to decide how to handle this new development. *Play it cool, Leslie,* she told herself. "I thought you were coming to my apartment."

"This dye is rather messy. It would be better to have the papers treated elsewhere."

"Where?" Leslie asked, now faintly alarmed.

"A place I know. Move over—I'll drive us there. It's a little hard to find." Andrew Miller opened the car door and would have sat in her lap if Leslie hadn't quickly moved out of his way. The gear shift lever stabbed her legs as she slid across the passenger seat.

Leslie weighed her options. If she tried to run away from him now, he would have the papers and her car and could probably escape arrest. If she went along with him, he would undoubtedly let her go as soon as he had the material he wanted. In any case, Leslie didn't want to make him suspicious of her.

"I'd prefer to drive. You can give me directions," she said.

"No. It'll be much better if I drive."

"I hadn't counted on this," she said as he left the parking lot and drove east. He hadn't bothered to adjust the seat, and his knees stuck up grotesquely. Thinking that he looked like a grown man trying to ride a child's bicycle, Leslie stifled an urge to giggle. *How can I laugh at a time like this?* Aware that she might be on the verge of hysteria, Leslie forced herself to take deep, calming breaths. She couldn't afford to lose control now.

Mr. Miller remained silent, concentrating on driving through the heavy Friday evening traffic. He didn't handle her car's manual transmission well, and Leslie winced as the gears protested each time he shifted. After several turns they reached a road that soon began to wind around the side of the mountain.

"Is this Monte Sano?" Leslie asked. "It doesn't look familiar."

"We're on the Bankhead Parkway. It goes up the back side of the mountain."

"Oh, I see. Do you live up here?"

"No," he said, and fell silent again.

Leslie glanced at the lighted dials on her dash, trying to see the fuel gauge. She knew she couldn't have much gas left; she usually filled her car as part of her regular Saturday chores. She didn't know which would be worse, to run out of gas and be stuck on the side of this lonely road with Andrew Miller, or to get to wherever he was taking her. And why had he insisted on using her car? Leslie decided it was a reasonable question.

"Is something wrong with your car?"

"My car?" he repeated, as if he hadn't understood her question.

"I'd think you'd prefer to drive your own car up here. Mine seems to be giving you some trouble."

He ignored her. When they reached the top of the mountain he turned into a narrow gravel road. Leslie tried to watch for landmarks, but in the darkness it was hard to make out the few signs they came across.

"It isn't very far now," he said after they had jolted over a particularly bad rut in the road. Leslie winced as her transmission groaned at his attempt to force it into a lower gear. "Perhaps you understand now why I wanted to drive," he said as he pulled into another, narrower lane, almost overgrown on both sides with underbrush and now-scarlet sumac.

At least I know how to shift the gears, Leslie thought, but stayed quiet. The last thing she should do would be to antagonize this strange man. She would hand over the papers and let him do whatever he would with them, then she'd get home as fast as she could—that was her revised agenda for the evening. Jack Taylor and the FBI would just have to catch Andrew Miller without any further help from her.

"Here we are," he said a few minutes later. He stopped beside a weatherbeaten frame cabin perched on the edge of the mountain. Except for a motorcycle parked to one side, there was little evidence that anyone had been there in years. Far below, the lights of the city twinkled in a panorama that under ordinary circumstances Leslie would have found breathtaking. Tonight she barely glanced at the view as Andrew Miller fumbled with a lock on the cabin door.

"Stay where you are until I can light the lantern," he directed when he finally opened the door. He struck a match to the wick, his face sinister in the shadowy light. The lamp smoked a little, then the flame took hold and burned brightly as he replaced the chimney and set the lamp down on a table.

"Is this where the FBI usually hangs out?" Leslie couldn't resist asking.

The man gave her a sharp glance and did not answer. Looking around, Leslie noted that the room contained a makeshift table and two ramshackle chairs that looked as if they might collapse if anyone tried to sit on them. Against one wall stood an army cot, neatly made up with a blanket and pillow. There was a closed door to the rear of the cabin which could lead to another room or outside.

"This is a strange place to transact business," Leslie said. She tried to overcome the feeling of dread that had followed her up the mountain, but the dismal place to which she had been led only made her more apprehensive. Why had she ever agreed to this wild scheme in the first place? And she must have been insane to allow him to bring her here.

"But it's very private. The papers, Miss Christopher?"

Leslie put her briefcase beside the lamp on the rickety table and reached into her purse for the key. Mr. Miller watched closely as she opened the lock and withdrew the papers. Handing them over, Leslie was grateful that the dim lantern light wouldn't allow him to make a very thorough inspection. She had fabricated several pages that could pass as the genuine article, but the others wouldn't fool anyone who had ever seen an engineering proposal.

"Is this all?" he asked, rifling through the slender stack.

"It's what you asked for," she replied steadily. "Now if you'll just go ahead and use the dye, I'd like to get home."

"Oh? Perhaps someone is waiting for you there?" His tone chilled her to the bone, and instinctively Leslie shuddered.

"What do you mean?"

"I mean I know all about Hampton Travis," he said smoothly. "He thought he could fool both of us, but it didn't work."

"I don't know what you're talking about," Leslie said. She devoutly wished that she had never challenged him. The lamplight made the glint in the man's eyes look even more evil.

"I believe you," he said with a faint half-smile. "In fact, Miss Christopher, there are a great many things that you don't know. That's why it's so totally unacceptable that you were put in charge of the VIRCO project."

"What?"

"You're a woman and you're much too young. I don't care how many hotshot things you did for Arrow in California, VIRCO should have gone to a man with experience and maturity, who knows Arrow/South inside and out."

"Someone like you, perhaps?" Leslie said as the last piece of the puzzle fell into place. She recalled how both Mr. Meredith and Sally had implied that she had won the job over local applicants. And Sally had mentioned that one of the men who had been passed over had left Arrow—

"Of course! It's really too bad that Arrow made the mistake of hiring a clumsy young woman with little enough sense in her pretty head to try to sell the company's secrets."

"What are you saying!" Leslie exclaimed, now genuinely alarmed.

"I'm saying that anyone with little enough sense to do what you've done could quite easily fall off the side of this mountain. Of course it could be a very long time before anyone thinks to look up here for you. They might not even bother to look at all, since they'll be sure you sold out to the highest bidder and took the money and ran. You might never be found," he finished, smiling as if the thought gave him a great deal of pleasure.

"You must be insane," Leslie said, her helplessness causing her to abandon caution. He had made her fate very plain. She had to see to it that he wouldn't be able to carry out his plans for her. But how?

He laughed without humor. "No one ever accused good old Jim Roberts of insanity. 'Good old Jim will do it,' Arrow always said when they wanted a job done right. And good old Jim always did what they wanted. But do you know what, Miss Christopher?

"After a while good old Jim wanted more than a pat on the back. It's hard to work for a company for half your life and wind up with nothing to show for it."

"You deserved to be promoted, even before the VIRCO project, didn't you?" Leslie questioned. She believed that as long as he was talking about himself, he wouldn't be likely to make a move against her. And maybe if he talked long enough, Leslie could figure a way to escape.

"Of course I deserved it!" he exclaimed.

"And when Arrow wouldn't pay you what you were worth, you started going to other companies with information about its projects?"

He allowed himself a small chuckle. "Even a stupid young woman like you can see that clear as day, right? All a man has is his work. No one—and certainly no *woman*—ought to be allowed to take that from him."

"Oh, I agree," Leslie said, slowly edging toward the table. If she could get near enough to push her briefcase, she could knock the lantern off the table and distract him long enough to get away. He had pocketed her car keys after he'd taken the briefcase out of the trunk, but that didn't matter. She would gladly walk all the way back down the mountain to escape this madman.

"Anyone but the fools at Arrow can see it wasn't fair," he began, looking at Leslie's face instead of her hands. Quickly she lunged toward the table and pushed the briefcase as hard as she could. It didn't slide well enough on the rough table top to knock the lamp to the floor; instead, the lamp merely teetered back and forth for a moment, then steadied, its flame barely disturbed.

His face contorted with rage, Jim Roberts grabbed Leslie's left wrist with such force that she cried out in pain.

"Oh, you think you're so smart, don't you? Let's see how smart you really are, Miss Christopher."

Still gripping her arm tightly, Roberts pushed open the back door and dragged her outside. The cold night air hit her face like a slap, clearing her head. Leslie remembered a move she'd learned in a self-defense course she'd taken. If done correctly she could throw a man twice her weight. She thought she could still do it, but first she had to make her captor grip her more closely. If she struggled the right way, perhaps he would.

"You know you can't get away with this," she said, trying to dig her high-heeled shoes in the soft earth.

"I already have," he said, jerking her after him. "Your FBI friends are sitting around in your apartment, waiting to spring their stupid trap. Won't they be surprised to find that their little decoy has flown the coop."

"How do you know that?" Leslie asked.

He chuckled evilly. "Surveillance can work both ways, you know."

"You mentioned Hampton Travis," Leslie said. "What do you know about him?"

"I said I fooled him and I did," Roberts replied. "He's probably right there with old Jack Taylor and the others at this very minute."

"Hampton Travis works for the FBI?" Leslie asked. His evil laugh, her reply.

"He fooled you good, didn't he? He and that stuck-up girl friend of his that works in Security."

"Barbara Redmond," Leslie said, not surprised. *So they do work together,* she thought. If Hampton was in love with someone else, surely he wouldn't have kissed her the way he had—

With a sudden sense of panic, Leslie saw that they were almost to the edge of the mountain, and she reached out and hooked her right arm around a slender tree. She hung on to it with all her might as Roberts continued to pull at her other arm, at first unaware of what she had done.

"You're just making it harder on yourself," he said, twisting her left arm until tears came into her eyes. "Let go of that tree."

As she did, Leslie bent double, made a fist with her right hand, and swung as hard as she could. His surprised cry of pain told her that she had hit her target, and as he reflexively relaxed his hold on her arm, she wrenched away from him.

Leslie ran around the side of the cabin and down the lane that led to the road. If he pursued her, she'd go into the woods and try to lose him in the thick undergrowth. Aware that her high heels slowed her progress, she kicked them off. She felt pain as sticks and rocks poked through her stockings, but she kept running anyway.

She thought she had gone as far as she possibly could without resting when a motorcycle roared to life. At the sound, Leslie crashed on into the dark woods, trying to avoid the motorcycle's probing headlight. She half-ran, half-walked until a stitch in her side bent her double and forced her to stop. Her lungs felt as if they would burst, every breath bringing new agony. She crouched behind a fallen log and tried to recover her breath.

The sound of the motorcycle was never far away. Sometimes it grew fainter, but she could always hear it. It would only be a matter of time until he found her; he knew she hadn't left the area. Her only chance of escape was to press on and hope to reach a safe hiding place before his motorcycle headlight could pinpoint her.

After a few moments, Leslie left her hiding place and continued walking. She decided not to run unless she was in immediate danger—there was too much risk of falling in the darkness. If she sprained her ankle—or worse—it would all be over. She shivered, not entirely from the cold. Leslie had no doubt that Jim Roberts was deranged enough to be capable of tossing her off the mountain without a second thought.

But first he would have to find her. Ironically enough, in all the turmoil of her thoughts, a snatch of a psalm came into Leslie's mind. *I will lift up mine eyes unto the hills, from whence cometh my help.*

Well, tonight this mountain was the site of her destruction, not her deliverance. Leslie walked on for several minutes, each seeming an eternity. She'd thought she was bearing away from the cabin, but suddenly she saw it through the trees on her left and realized she'd been walking in a circle.

"Lost people bear to the left," Hampton had said that golden day when they had gone hiking on this very mountain.

Thinking of him gave Leslie a temporary lift. Whoever he was, an FBI agent as Roberts had implied, or just a man who had given up a job with Arrow for her sake, Leslie knew that Hampton Travis meant a great deal to her.

What would Hampton do if he were in my place? she asked herself. Almost immediately, recalling the quiet strength of his faith, Leslie knew that Hampton would probably have started praying a long time ago. And while she wasn't accustomed to it, Leslie was desperate enough to try it. Standing where she was, Leslie shut her eyes and spoke earnestly, almost whispering.

Lord, I'm not very good at this prayer business, but I do believe that You can help me, and You certainly know I need help. As an afterthought, Leslie added "Amen" and opened her eyes just as the sound of the motorcycle grew increasingly louder.

A feeling of the most intense peace she had ever experienced flooded over Leslie like a benediction, but she didn't have time to consider its source or what it meant. Over her shoulder Leslie saw the headlight beaming through the trees, heading straight toward her. Summoning a final burst of energy, Leslie ran toward the cabin, lurched inside, closed and leaned against the door, panting for breath.

She heard the motorcycle engine cut off and the footsteps in the cabin porch. Quickly she grabbed one of the chairs and raised it high as a dark shape entered the cabin. Leslie brought the chair down as hard as she could on the side of Jim Roberts' head, and he fell forward with a muffled groan. Quickly she bent to search his pockets for her car keys. She had them in hand and had turned to leave when a new set of headlights appeared in the narrow lane.

What next! she thought. Casting a wary eye on Roberts, who seemed to be out of it for the time being, Leslie went out of the rear door and crouched behind the cabin as an automobile pulled up behind hers and stopped. She heard car doors opening and closing, followed by footsteps on the cabin porch, then a loud exclamation.

"Here's Roberts, but I don't see the girl."

Then Leslie's eyes widened and her breath caught in her throat as a voice she instantly recognized called her name. She made her way to the back door of the cabin and sagged against the door frame, feeling suddenly faint.

"Here I am," she said weakly.

Hampton turned, and Leslie knew she would always remember how he looked, silhouetted in the lantern light as he reached out to her and held her as if he never intended to let her go.

"I've never been so glad to see anyone in my life," Leslie said when she could speak again. "I won't even ask what you're doing here."

"I'm rescuing you, of course," Hampton said. He continued to hold Leslie tightly until she winced and pulled away from him.

"My arm seems to be a bit skinned," she said apologetically.

"Thank heaven we got here in time," the first voice she had heard said, and Leslie looked past Hampton to see Jack Taylor handcuffing the awakening figure on the floor.

"God heard me—I haven't prayed that hard since that shuttle flight when we had to make an emergency landing."

"He told me you work for the FBI," Leslie said to Hampton. "Why didn't you tell me?"

"I couldn't." Hampton led Leslie closer to the lamp and inspected her arm. "Jack, look at her arm—we need to get Leslie to the hospital right away."

Jack Taylor walked over to inspect her arm and nodded in agreement. "I'm afraid that'll take some stitching."

"I'm not hurt all that much," Leslie protested, but she allowed Hampton to pick her up and carry her to the car as Jack Taylor brought Roberts out and put him in the other car.

Using his cellular phone, Jack Taylor made a call. "Barbara? You can leave the apartment now. The suspect is in custody and Miss Christopher is safe."

"Barbara?" Leslie repeated, looking quizzically at Hampton. "She's at my apartment?"

"We all were for a while," Hampton replied with his best smile. "It was quite a party."

"Nobody invited me," Leslie said.

"It's not our fault you ran out on us."

"Or mine, either. That man had other plans for me."

Hampton put his arms around Leslie and kissed her tenderly. "Thank God he didn't get to carry them out."

Leslie glanced back at her captor. He sat in the backseat of Taylor's car, his head down. Despite all he had put her through, Leslie felt stirred by a strange sense of pity.

"What will happen to him now?" she asked.

"That's up to the Federal courts, but he'll likely be charged with abduction and assault, in addition to whatever Arrow slaps him with."

Leslie sighed. "Poor man. He wanted my job."

"And your life," Hampton reminded her.

As they followed Jack Taylor's car down the mountain, Hampton kept glancing over at Leslie as if he couldn't bear to let her out of his sight, even for a moment. Despite the throbbing pain in her arm, Leslie felt content just to be with Hampton again and to know how he felt about her.

"You gave us quite a scare, young lady." He reached out and brushed a twig from her hair with his free hand.

"I was pretty scared there for awhile myself," she admitted. "But a strange thing happened when I realized that I might not be able to get away from him." She stopped, suddenly shy talking about how she had felt when she had prayed for deliverance.

"I think I can guess what it was," Hampton said. "I can see that in all of this you've been touched by the Lord."

"Can you?" Leslie pulled down the sun visor and looked at her scratched face. "It looks more like I was touched by a porcupine."

"I'm right, though?" he persisted, and Leslie nodded.

"I can't describe it—I was so tired I didn't think I could take another step, and he was coming after me—and I knew he meant to throw me over the side of the mountain—then I just asked God to help me, and He did. The next thing I knew, I was able to sprint to the cabin."

Hampton nodded as if he understood exactly what had happened. "It's a little scary, isn't it?"

"Not as scary as what almost happened. He was going to let everyone think I'd been selling information from Arrow."

"I know," Hampton said. "I prayed that we'd reach you in time, but you and God were obviously doing pretty well on your own."

"I guess the secret of good management is knowing who to get to do a job," Leslie said, attempting a weak smile. "But seriously, I didn't know you were back in Huntsville—and how did you know where to find me? I didn't even know where I was, myself."

"I came back because my work in California was finished, and I knew whoever was trying to get the VIRCO information would act soon. My plane got in about four-thirty and I went directly to your apartment, where Jack and Barbara were waiting. They filled me in on what was happening with you and Jim Roberts. When you hadn't shown up by six o'clock, they knew something had gone wrong."

"But I still don't know how you knew I was up here."

"I put a tail on your car before I went to California, a gizmo that sends a message to a satellite, which is then beamed back to earth at an assigned frequency. It led us straight to you."

Leslie shivered. "He drove my car up here, even though I tried to talk him out of it."

"It's a good thing he didn't listen to you."

"What made you think that I might need protection?"

"We knew that whoever was selling secrets would probably try to get them on VIRCO."

Still confused, Leslie frowned. "Is that why you wanted to be assigned to VIRCO?"

"That was the original plan. But for several reasons—including a very personal one—I decided to let Barbara keep an eye out for you instead."

"I always hoped that you were on the right side all along," Leslie said despondently, "but I've been so stupid—"

"Here, here, there'll be none of that!" Hampton stopped for a traffic signal and leaned over to kiss her cheek lightly. "You don't have the corner on stupidity. I should have suspected Roberts from the start, but we thought he'd left town."

"Oh, Hampton," Leslie began, but he touched her lips gently with his free hand.

"Hush."

"But—" Leslie began again.

"Later. Here's the hospital. They'll probably think I've been battering you," he said as one of the emergency attendants came out with a wheelchair.

"What happened to you, honey?" the admitting clerk asked. "You look like you fell off the mountain."

"Almost," Leslie replied. She shuddered again, thinking how close she had come to disaster. "I seem to have a few scratches and bruises."

"Abrasions and contusions," the nurse said. Leslie and Hampton exchanged smiles.

"Wait here," the nurse instructed Hampton as Leslie was wheeled away for treatment.

He'd barely had time to drink a cup of cool vending machine coffee before Leslie returned, sporting several stitches in her right arm and bandages on the worst of her leg wounds.

"She'll live," the young emergency room doctor told Hampton. "I'd keep her off the mountain for a spell, though."

"I'll try, but you know how flighty these females can

get sometimes."

"If I felt better, I'd hit you," Leslie said as Hampton helped her into her car.

"I don't think you're going to be hitting anything for a while. You really do look awful."

"Thanks a lot," Leslie said.

When they reached her apartment, Leslie lay on the sofa and Hampton sat cross-legged on the floor facing her. "I should go now and let you get some sleep," he said, but she shook her head.

"Stay a little while, anyway. I haven't seen you in so long, I'd almost forgotten what you looked like."

Aware that she was teasing him, Hampton smiled and took one of her hands in his. "I've been doing some serious thinking lately," he told her.

"About what?" Leslie asked. With her hand in his, Leslie felt at ease for the first time in almost as long as she could remember.

"A lot of things, but mostly about you. My work has always been important to me, and I never backed out of an assignment in my life. But as soon as I met you, I knew that if I had to choose between seeing you and infiltrating Arrow, it was no choice at all."

"Why didn't you tell me what you were up to from the start?"

"I couldn't. It would have endangered the whole operation and especially you."

Leslie sighed. "I must be the most lied-to person in this town. How can I ever believe anyone again after this?"

Hampton sat beside her on the sofa and brushed her lips lightly with his. "Do you believe that?"

Leslie reached her hand out to touch his face, allowing

her fingers to caress the cleft in his chin and explore the corners of his mouth. "I'm not sure I can," she whispered before his lips closed on hers once more, and he kissed her gently but passionately.

"You can trust me forever and ever," he said as he pulled back and looked into her eyes.

"That's a long time," she said, and he kissed her again.

"A lifetime, as a matter of fact. The important thing is that I love you, my dearest Leslie, and I think you just might feel the same way about me."

Tears came to Leslie's eyes, and she nodded, unable to speak.

"Then you will start to thinking about marrying me, I hope?"

Leslie smiled. "But I've just found a wonderful singles group at Glenview—"

"Really? I understand they have wonderful couples' classes too."

"We would be a couple, wouldn't we?" Leslie said with wonder. "Will you stay on in Huntsville permanently, then?"

Hampton kissed her lightly on the nose. "You're tired. We'll talk about all of that later."

"How wonderful it is to have a 'later,'" Leslie murmured against his cheek.

"All the laters in our lifetime," he assured her.

As Hampton's arms tightened around her once more, Leslie knew that she had found what she had been searching for all her life, without even knowing what she sought. At last she had the promise of the security she had been missing.

"It's all a matter of security," she murmured.

Hampton looked at her and smiled. "What is?"

"Us," Leslie replied, knowing she made no sense but unable to express the feelings that crowded her heart.

In reply, Hampton gathered her to him again and Leslie sighed in contentment.

Having the security of her and Hampton's love throughout their life would be wonderful; but God had also offered Leslie another, more important security.

She had glimpsed it briefly at Glenview and then fully realized it in her desperate prayer in the woods—Leslie also had the promise of God's security, which far surpassed any human love and which would last for all eternity.

epilogue

"I don't think this chapel is big enough to hold everyone who wants to see you and Hampton get married," Sally said minutes before the organist was scheduled to play Mendelsohn's "Wedding March." Sally had just looked through the peephole in the Glenview Chapel Bride's Room, and when she turned to Leslie, her face glowing with excitement.

"I hope the security people we hired will keep out the TV cameras," Leslie said.

"That's the price you have to pay for being a celebrity," Sally replied only half teasing. In the six months since Leslie's abduction, the tabloid press had had a field day with the story of an ex-astronaut who had come to the rescue of a beautiful young woman bravely working as an undercover agent to help the FBI apprehend a spy.

"Hampton once told me he'd had his fill of being in the spotlight—now I know what he meant."

"But at least some good came of it. What a great testimony you and Hampton gave to the millions of people who heard you praise God for helping you through it!"

"Right now I'm only concerned about one person," Leslie said. "Despite that old superstition about brides and grooms not seeing each other on the day of the wedding, I'd feel a lot better if I could have talked to Hampton today."

"Well, for the record I did see him. Other than saying

he's more nervous today than he was on his first trip into space, Dr. Travis seems to be holding up well."

"What about Pat? How is he holding up?" Leslie asked, unable to resist teasing her matron of honor about the man that had become an increasingly important part of her life.

"Your wedding has set us both to thinking that maybe our getting married wouldn't be such a bad idea."

"I can hear Dale now, complaining that he's losing all his singles class to matrimony," Leslie said with a smile. "What's happening out there now?" she added, hearing a different tune from the organ.

Sally turned back to the keyhole. "Hampton's mother is being seated. You can sure tell she lives in Florida—she has a great tan. Now here come Pastor Carew and Hampton and his father. Hampton looks a little pale."

"Where's my bouquet?" Leslie asked, temporarily losing her fine edge of organization and order.

"Right here," Sally said. She handed it to Leslie as a light rap sounded on the door, and Richard Meredith, looking splendid in his morning coat, beckoned to them.

"I think I'm supposed to walk you down the aisle for some reason or the other," he said lightly. Gratefully Leslie took his arm.

"You look very nice, sir," Leslie said.

"So do you," he returned.

In her simple white satin gown, adorned only by a string of pearls from Hampton, Leslie didn't know if she was beautiful, but the joy that she felt sure made her feel radiant.

The first strains of the wedding march swept through the Glenview chapel. Sally gave the thumbs-up sign to

Leslie and turned to walk slowly down the aisle, where groomsman Pat Wentworth watched her with obvious admiration.

"Shall we?" Mr. Meredith asked.

Forcing herself to walk slowly, Leslie began to move down the aisle, her eyes fixed on Hampton's.

As soon as he saw her, Hampton broke into a broad grin. Leslie smiled, overwhelmed by her feelings of gratitude. With a full heart she acknowledged that the things that had happened to her since her arrival in Huntsville— capturing Jim Roberts, her successful management of Arrow's VIRCO proposal, her love for Hampton Travis, and, most especially, the security of her salvation—had all been part of God's plan for her life.

At last she reached the altar and Mr. Meredith handed her over to Hampton. He gripped her hand tightly and looked down at her with such a look of love that Leslie almost wept from the emotion enveloping her.

"Let us pray," Pastor Carew said. Gratefully Leslie bowed her head. *Thank you, Lord*, she said silently, and knew that Hampton was probably breathing the same prayer. *Help us always to remember this day and the feelings we share.*

As Leslie and Hampton exchanged their vows in voices that never wavered, she somehow knew that the God who had brought Hampton to her would help them stay together as they looked to Him for their security.

A Letter To Our Readers

Dear Reader:

In order that we might better contribute to your reading enjoyment, we would appreciate your taking a few minutes to respond to the following questions. When completed, please return to the following:

Rebecca Germany, Editor
Heartsong Presents
P.O. Box 719
Uhrichsville, Ohio 44683

1. Did you enjoy reading *A Matter of Security*?
   ❏ Very much. I would like to see more books
      by this author!
   ❏ Moderately
      I would have enjoyed it more if _____

   _____

2. Are you a member of *Heartsong Presents*? Yes   No
   If no, where did you purchase this book? _____

   _____

3. What influenced your decision to purchase this
   book? (Check those that apply.)

   ❏ Cover   ❏ Back cover copy

   ❏ Title   ❏ Friends

   ❏ Publicity   ❏ Other _____

4. On a scale from 1 (poor) to 10 (superior), please rate the following elements.

___Heroine ___Plot

___Hero ___Inspirational theme

___Setting ___Secondary characters

5. What settings would you like to see covered in *Heartsong Presents* books?

_____

_____

6. What are some inspirational themes you would like to see treated in future books?_____

_____

_____

7. Would you be interested in reading other *Heartsong Presents* titles? ❑ Yes ❑ No

8. Please check your age range:
❑ Under 18 ❑ 18-24 ❑ 25-34
❑ 35-45 ❑ 46-55 ❑ Over 55

9. How many hours per week do you read? _____

Name _____

Occupation _____

Address _____

City _____ State _____ Zip _____

Frontiers of Faith
Kay Cornelius

___Sign of the Bow___—Hours after the first warning of trouble, Sara Craighead, surrounded by Seneca warriors, is on a forced march through the dense woods. Her little brother was kidnapped by another group of Seneca, and Sarah has no idea whether her parents are dead or alive. HP87 $2.95

___Sign of the Eagle___—Young and strong, Adam leaves his wilderness home to discover what work God has called him to. Adam's long blond hair and buckskin clothing cut a dashing figure on Philadelphia's streets and attract attention from two of the most eligible young women in the city. HP91 $2.95

___Sign of the Dove___—As the end of war returns peace to Carolina, Hannah finds herself fighting a new battle in her heart. Not only must she determine her true feelings for Clay and Nate, but she also must resolve the anger and bitterness she harbors toward her cousin Marie. HP95 $2.95

___Sign of the Spirit___—Coming Soon!

·····Heart♥ng·····

Any 12
Heartsong
Presents titles
for only
$26.95 *

CONTEMPORARY ROMANCE IS CHEAPER BY THE DOZEN!

Buy any assortment of twelve *Heartsong Presents* titles and save 25% off of the already discounted price of $2.95 each!

*plus $1.00 shipping and handling per order and sales tax where applicable.

HEARTSONG PRESENTS TITLES AVAILABLE NOW:

*Temporarily out of stock.

(If ordering from this page, please remember to include it with the order form.)

·······Presents·······

*Temporarily out of stock.

Great Inspirational Romance at a Great Price!

Heartsong Presents books are inspirational romances in contemporary and historical settings, designed to give you an enjoyable, spirit-lifting reading experience. You can choose from 132 wonderfully written titles from some of today's best authors like Colleen L. Reece, Brenda Bancroft, Janelle Jamison, and many others.

When ordering quantities less than twelve, above titles are $2.95 each.

Heartsong Presents
Love Stories Are Rated G!

That's for godly, gratifying, and of course, great! If you love a thrilling love story, but don't appreciate the sordidness of popular paperback romances, **Heartsong Presents** is for you. In fact, **Heartsong Presents** is the *only inspirational romance book club*, the only one featuring love stories where Christian faith is the primary ingredient in a marriage relationship.

Sign up today to receive your first set of four, never before published Christian romances. Send no money now; you will receive a bill with the first shipment. You may cancel at any time without obligation, and if you aren't completely satisfied with any selection, you may return the books for an immediate refund!

Imagine. . .four new romances every month—two historical, two contemporary—with men and women like you who long to meet the one God has chosen as the love of their lives. . .all for the low price of $9.97 postpaid.

To join, simply complete the coupon below and mail to the address provided. **Heartsong Presents** romances are rated G for another reason: They'll arrive *Godspeed!*